THE VIRGIN GIFT

LAUREN BLAKELY

COPYRIGHT

ALSO BY LAUREN BLAKELY

Big Rock Series

Big Rock

Mister O

Well Hung

Full Package

Joy Ride

Hard Wood

One Love Series

The Sexy One

The Only One

The Hot One

The Knocked Up Plan

Come As You Are

The Heartbreakers Series

Once Upon a Real Good Time

Once Upon a Sure Thing

Once Upon a Wild Fling

Sports Romance

Most Valuable Playboy

Most Likely to Score

Lucky In Love Series

Best Laid Plans

The Feel Good Factor

Nobody Does It Better

Unzipped

Always Satisfied Series

Satisfaction Guaranteed

Instant Gratification

Overnight Service

Never Have I Ever

Special Delivery

The Gift Series

The Engagement Gift

The Virgin Gift

The Decadent Gift (coming soon)

Standalone

Stud Finder

The V Card

Wanderlust

Part-Time Lover

The Real Deal

Unbreak My Heart

The Break-Up Album

21 Stolen Kisses

Out of Bounds

Birthday Suit

The Dating Proposal

The Caught Up in Love Series

Caught Up In Us

Pretending He's Mine

Playing With Her Heart

Stars In Their Eyes Duet

My Charming Rival

My Sexy Rival

The No Regrets Series

The Thrill of It

The Start of Us

Every Second With You

The Seductive Nights Series

First Night (Julia and Clay, prequel novella)

Night After Night (Julia and Clay, book one)

After This Night (Julia and Clay, book two)

One More Night (Julia and Clay, book three)

A Wildly Seductive Night (Julia and Clay novella, book 3.5)

The Joy Delivered Duet

Nights With Him (A standalone novel about Michelle and Jack)

Forbidden Nights (A standalone novel about Nate and Casey)

The Sinful Nights Series

Sweet Sinful Nights

Sinful Desire

Sinful Longing

Sinful Love

The Fighting Fire Series

Burn For Me (Smith and Jamie)

Melt for Him (Megan and Becker)

Consumed By You (Travis and Cara)

The Jewel Series

A two-book sexy contemporary romance series

The Sapphire Affair

The Sapphire Heist

ABOUT

I might be a virgin, but I know what I want in bed. It's just that I haven't found him yet.

So I'm stunned when charming, laid-back Adam volunteers to work through my sexual wish list. That's when I discover the voracious, filthy-mouthed, after-dark alpha in him, my next door neighbor. And I'm enthralled -- in and out of the bedroom.

Every night we explore my fantasies, and every morning I try harder not to want more from him. Because there's no item on my list about falling for the guy. Besides, we agreed to the final item already -- when we're done we walk away.

But every fantasy unlocks another. Each hotter than the last. Until I discover there's one last thing on my to-do list to check off. One so forbidden I can't figure out how to ask him or what it might to do my heart...

THE VIRGIN GIFT

Want to be the first to learn of sales, new releases, preorders and special freebies? Sign up for my VIP mailing list here! This will ensure that you're the first to know when new After Dark books go live special release day prices!

1

NINA

From my vantage point, I saw it all.

I watched the prelude to every fantasy unfold. I witnessed women luxuriating in their bodies and men wrapping their arms around them—lovers poised with coiled tension, a powder keg of desire primed to explode.

I gazed at women and women, men and women, men and men. And women alone, desire written in their eyes.

Today, from behind the lens, I studied a party of two, drenched in sexual anticipation.

In my studio, the curvy brunette stretched like a cat across the sapphire-blue cover on the opulent bed. The dark-haired man gripped her hip with one hand, his other in her hair. He lay behind her, his body sealed to hers, his eyes hooded.

A queen flanked by her loyal soldier, who served and protected her. Or maybe she served him. As I snapped shot after shot, I wrote the script to their after-dark affairs, imagining filthy moment after filthy moment.

Truth be told, I didn't have to imagine much. Their passion for each other was evident in their expressions, unmistakable in the tangling of their limbs. Yes, I'd posed them in my studio boudoir, but the poses came so naturally to these two.

I moved around the bed, giving direction from my Nikon. "Marco, can you move your hand down her thigh a little bit? I want to see more of the curve of Evangeline's sexy hip."

"It is the sexiest hip God ever created," he growled, making the adjustment.

"And, Evangeline, look to the left so the camera can see more of those glossy pink lips."

She shifted, briefly shooting him a look, a private gaze.

So much was unsaid in the way they stole glances at each other.

Longing. Craving. Heat.

My mind raced ahead.

Would he take her after their photo session? Would his hands travel all over her lush body?

I wrote Marco and Evangeline's afternoon delight in my head.

Perhaps my neighbors would tell stories later of how the lift was stuck for thirty minutes that afternoon, and it was *sooo* annoying to have a mechanical malfunction.

Only I'd know what had really happened.

I'd know why everyone in this high-rise had to take the stairs.

The second they left my home studio and entered the elevator down the hall, Marco would become insatiable, his palm slamming against the stop button. He'd yank up her skirt and thrust inside her, her wrists pinned above her head. She'd need no coaxing. She'd be ready for him, head thrown back, lips parted, taking it hard and loving it.

Or perhaps the legend of their passion would be written in the parking garage. Maybe he'd pounce on her in the front seat before they turned on the engine, and those coming home early from work would do a double take.

Did you see them? That couple heating up the windows in the black Audi? She rode him like he was her stallion.

Or maybe they'd play denial games on the drive back to their home.

Evangeline would want to touch herself, and Marco would issue orders in a deep, rumbling voice, one hand on the steering wheel, one on her bare thigh.

Don't touch yourself till I say so.

Show me your panties.

Now show me yourself.

I bet she'd loved being told what to do.

Bet she craved it like air.

He'd make her squirm till they returned home and he'd order her to get down on all fours and then he'd take her to the edge of pleasure.

I clenched my thighs at the wild thoughts racing through my head as my camera captured their suggestive poses, their heated expressions, the sensual record of the moments before the camera stopped clicking.

Before.

That was what my lens recorded. The build, the slow burn, the seconds that ticked till these lovers lunged at each other.

Sensual boudoir photography was my jam.

It was the best job ever.

And also the worst.

Because of days like this. When my mind zigged and zagged with images.

But I was a professional, and I had to keep my own wild meanderings at bay and finish the job.

I zoomed in on their faces, then I stepped back, grabbing a series of full-body shots as the couple shifted, sitting up, her legs wrapped around his ass, their arms curled around each other. Two people who couldn't get enough of each other.

"Gorgeous," I said, murmuring my approval. "Now, Evangeline, I want you to look at Marco like you're going to rip off all his clothes."

She laughed, shooting me a playful glance. "But I've already stripped him down to his boxers."

I smiled knowingly from behind the camera. "Then you're not done. Look at him like you're going to tug those boxers off and have a field day with him."

"Field day," he whispered to her in a voice tinged with lust. "That's what we'll have when we're done."

Just as I predicted.

Then the pair of them laughed, and I caught that too, because that's what they'd asked for when they ordered this photoshoot—to record their love, their passion, and their trust in each other. They wanted it all for posterity

—when they longed for each other and when they laughed with each other too. They seemed to share their vulnerability and tenderness so easily in a stranger's bedroom. How did they do that? How did they let go?

"Just behave while you're in here," I teased. "But, Marco, I need one thing from you."

"Name it," the man said.

"Run your hands through her hair," I told him.

A groan rumbled up his chest so loud I could hear it. His fingers roped through her honey-brown strands, and I snapped that shot, capturing provocative moment after provocative moment, even as my mind ran away again.

I wanted *that*. Wanted it for me, and wanted it for my damn job. If only so I could get these images out of my head while I worked.

Surely my overactive, overheated imagination helped my job of capturing sensuality. But I didn't need dirty images bearing down in the studio. And the images showed no signs of abating as I pictured his hands tightening around her glossy locks later, tugging, pulling, yanking.

Did he make her scream?

Moan?

Or simply melt?

All of the above, I decided as they cast hot stares at each other. The longing in her eyes was visceral, a palpable force in the room. In his irises, I saw intense devotion and filthy desire. This was when I stopped directing them, letting their natural instincts take over.

She pressed her body closer to her man, sealing herself to him like she was riding him.

"I want something that captures us in the throes of passion," she said, her voice smoky, like she could barely hold back as she looked at me. "Nina, do I look like a woman about to be devoured?"

I answered her with complete honesty. "Yes."

A small smile seemed to tease at her lips. "Best feeling ever, isn't it?" She winked, like we were soul sisters on this front.

I answered her with a total lie. "Of course."

Inside, I replied truthfully, privately, saying, *I wouldn't know.*

I've never had what she's having.

* * *

Evangeline pulled on a robe as Marco excused himself to the restroom to dress.

It was funny to see his modesty after I'd already witnessed him so exposed—though not physically. I never captured full nudes of men. Only women, and only if they requested.

But I was grateful he was gone for a few minutes, because I found it easier to show women the images on the back of the camera without their lovers by their side. She could look at them through her own eyes, not his.

And women saw their bodies differently than men did.

Mostly women saw the emotions in the photos, not

simply the beautiful bodies. That was what I always tried to convey in both the solo shoots of women and the couple shoots—the *emotions*.

Evangeline couldn't contain a wildly pleased grin as she stared at the window on my camera.

"You're very good," she said, cooing at the shots, almost tracing her finger against the screen. "I've never seen us look this way before. Our faces caught in these moments . . . moments of passion."

I smiled. That's what I loved most about my job—when my clients were comfortable enough to relax and let go, to reveal to the camera what was so rarely seen in front of others.

But I wasn't going to take credit for their desire.

"The two of you make it easy," I said, deflecting the attention to the client, where it belonged. "You're obviously so deeply in love."

I expected her to murmur a quiet *thank you* or to simply agree, giving me a *yes, we are*.

But her answer took me by surprise as she looked away from the camera and met my gaze. "It's not easy. It took me a long time to get to this place."

I tilted my head, curious. "What do you mean?"

Her brown eyes were rich with secret knowledge, insight into the ways of sensuality. "To ask for what I wanted."

"You weren't able to before?" I was eager to understand what she meant. I wanted to know how to ask for that. I wanted to have that.

"No. I was terrible with communication in my early twenties. I was unsure of my own desires. I didn't know what I needed in bed, and in love, and in life. And then I learned how to speak about my desires."

"How?" The word hung in the air, a desperate plea. "What did it for you?"

She moved in closer, like she was about to impart the kind of secret passed down through generations, protected by a secret society. "*Aphrodite*. She changed my life."

"The ancient Greek goddess? Have you been visiting Mount Olympus?" I asked with a light laugh.

She answered with a chuckle, but shook her head. "Please. You don't have to go beyond these four walls to visit with her. And she is a modern-day goddess. A goddess of sensuality. I'll introduce you to her."

I blinked, trying to figure out if my client was talking in code or truly believed she could speak with mythological figures. But I was intrigued enough to keep going. "How would I find Aphrodite?"

"Do you have a smartphone?"

I laughed and couldn't resist rolling my eyes. "No," I teased as I reached for the mobile device in my jeans pocket. "Of course I do."

"And do you have a podcast app?" Evangeline asked, and the puzzle pieces started to slide into place. She wasn't in touch with ancient Greek gods and goddesses, but rather the world of podcasts. I was down with that.

"Yes. I love science podcasts and how stuff works podcasts," I said, brightening as I thought of my collection of "Geeks R Us" podcasts, as my friend Lily playfully referred to my listening addiction.

"File this under how stuff works, then," she said with

a twinkle in her eyes as she tapped on the screen, then showed me the artwork for *Ask Aphrodite*. Ah, that made sense. "I swear you won't regret it. Aphrodite changed my life. I learned how to ask for what I want in bed. And Marco gives it to me. Now, thanks to her, I know what it's like to feel incredible, to have a lover take me to the edge of desire." She sighed seductively as if remembering that feeling. "To the edge and beyond." Then she collected herself. "You know what that's like. That kind of O."

She said it absently, offhand, even, as she turned around and picked up her clothes.

I smiled and gave a quiet "Yes."

But the truth was, I knew nothing of the sort.

When they left, I shut the door, a heaviness in my chest from telling another half-truth.

I didn't lie all day long. Some days no one asked about me. But questions from clients arose more often than not, peppered with knowing glances and sisters-in-sensual-arms winks. And I wanted to stop telling little white lies in my studio. I wanted to have one full, honest conversation with a client when she'd ask about sex, or desire, or longing.

Color me a contradiction.

I was the boudoir photographer who'd never been naked with a man before.

The more I shot, the more I wanted to know what the couples in my photos were feeling.

Wait. Correction: the more I *needed* to know.

2

NINA

With Marco and Evangeline banging in the elevator or screwing in the car, I popped in my AirPods and toggled over to my podcast app to learn the inner workings of black holes, then attached my camera to my computer to download the photos.

But as the host explained that a black hole is a region in space where the force of gravity is so strong that light can't escape, a notion published by scientist David Finkelstein in the 1950s, I hit stop.

I couldn't listen anymore.

My virginity was a black hole.

And I needed to escape from it.

And the longer the pull of gravity worked on my V card, the harder it would be to give it up.

And, in turn, to fully connect with my clients. To relate to them as a *woman in the know*. And then, once I was on that other secret side of knowledge, the images of their pleasure wouldn't tease me as I worked.

But there was more at play, of course. I wanted what they were having . . . *because.*

Because pleasure was its own motivation.

And I'd never experienced true pleasure from another person.

It was time.

Time to fully connect with my own desires—desires that had lived only in my mind.

Communication. That was what I needed. The few times I was involved with a man long enough that I thought it might lead to sex, I'd never known exactly how to bring up the nagging little issue of breaking my hymen. So I hadn't ventured down the roads that led out of virginity.

"Sorry, Finkelstein. It's time for the goddess," I said, and I hit download on the first episode of *Ask Aphrodite*, reading the description aloud.

"How to have the love life you deserve. A love and intimacy advice show with your hostess, Aphrodite, answering all your questions."

I had so many questions. I turned away from the computer, knowing I'd come back to Marco and Evangeline's passion soon enough.

For now, I gave Aphrodite my full attention as her voice filled my ears.

Hello there, gorgeous lovelies. Welcome to episode one of Ask Aphrodite. I'm your guide through the wilds of desire and sensuality, wherever you are in your journey. Ask any ques-

tion, and I'll endeavor to answer it, even if I have to dig far and wide.

But first, I want you to take the initial step on the path to knowing yourself, to understanding your fantasies, and perhaps to having them.

This is what I want you to do today.

Ask these questions and respond honestly. Only with honesty comes passion, intimacy, and incandescent bliss.

What do you want?

What thoughts and desires keep you awake at night?

What are the images that race through your mind when you're alone?

We all know secretly what gets us off. Think about your dirty dreams, and then put pen to paper, writing them down, knowing them, and in so doing, knowing yourself.

When the episode ended, I reached for one of my idea notebooks, with an illustrated owl on the cover. I kept one in each room, writing down my ideas for new poses, new shoots as they struck me.

This time, I wrote down something for me.

I began a list.

My filthy, wild list.

I started with one, then filled in a few more items until my phone pinged with a text from my friend and next-door neighbor.

Adam: Can I take you up on that offer for one more night? I'll make a chicken stir-fry as thanks tonight, and it'll be so delicious your taste buds will sing my praises for days.

Nina: Of course you can take me up on it. But seriously, my taste buds will *only* sing for days? You must be slacking. Last time you made me a pad thai so yummy my taste buds performed arias for weeks. Now I get mere days?

Adam: Do not doubt me, woman. I will ensure you're more than satisfied. Don't I always please you in the kitchen?

Nina: Hmm. Always? That's a powerful word. I'd say most of the time, because let's not ever forget the pumpkin chocolate chip cookie incident.

Adam: Oh, no, you don't. Do not go there. We made a vow to never bring that up again.

Nina: Did we now?

Adam: Yes. We swore you'd never bring up the worse-than-cardboard batch of cookies I made, and I'd never bring up the time you insisted the Hundred Years' War lasted one hundred years.

Nina: Everyone gets that wrong! It's a trick question.

Adam: And I was tricked by pumpkin. Everyone gets tricked by pumpkin. It's what happens every damn fall.

So let's agree to never mention the pumpkin chocolate chip cookies and I will keep that trivia faux pas under wraps.

Nina: *grumbles* Fine. I agree. Also, can't wait for the stir-fry. You are a master in the kitchen.

Adam: Can't wait to cook for you. Also, thanks, Nina. I appreciate it. I owe you big time.

Nina: You owe me nothing. Happy to help.

I set down the phone, a smile tugging on my lips. Adam had that effect on me, with his charming, laid-back ways, his easygoing personality.

I'd enjoyed having my friend spend the last few nights in my guest room. One more night of his cooking, his laughter, and our long chats into the night about how solar panel highways worked, or how long badly named wars lasted, or whether it was better to say "champing at the bit" or "chomping at the bit" would be fun.

He was always fun.

But I had other matters on my mind and steep hills to climb.

I returned to my list, doing as Aphrodite said.

By the time I was done, I had ten items, and the last one would be the hardest. Take the longest. Require the most work.

I didn't know where to start with that one, so I doodled next to it, drawing the outline of a fox, until an idea for one more dirty wish landed in my head.

The start of an eleventh. I began to write it down, but there was a knock on my door. A series of knocks, rapid, urgent, incessant. It sounded like someone was having an emergency.

3

ADAM

That was a prize-winning day.

Two deals done. Two clients made happy. And a new streaming show premiering next week.

Talk about a kick-ass ten hours at my production studio.

I left my office, lowered my shades to shield my eyes from the too-bright Vegas sun, and hit the key fob on my Tesla. As the door opened, I rated my day a B.

No, make that a B-plus.

It wasn't an A yet, because days didn't receive their final grades till night rolled around. Nighttime had a way of raising grades to A-pluses.

But when I checked my texts and found one from the painter, my shoulders sagged before I could even put the car in reverse.

David The Painter: *Still not done with the painting, Mr. Larkin. We should finish in two more days.*

And that made my day a C.

Fumes. Freaking paint fumes in my condo for another night.

I'd already overstayed my welcome at Nina's place, since she'd let me spend the last few nights there.

I didn't want to put her out again, even though it was no hardship staying with my witty, entertaining, sexy-as-hell neighbor. And I didn't say that simply because her guest room was better than most Vegas hotel rooms—the woman had impeccable taste and an eye for what made beds feel absolutely spectacular. I had no idea I'd like that many pillows to rest my head on, or such a top-of-the-line downy comforter.

But damn, her guest bed rocked.

No surprise, since she rocked.

Staying with her was a helluva way to spend the evenings. We clicked so well, it was as if we'd known each other forever rather than simply the last few years.

The only challenge? Nina was as tempting as the most decadent dessert, the kind you wanted to sneak a bite of when no one was looking.

A dark-haired angel with red cat-eye glasses, glossy lips, and a tight body. With her deadpan wit, locomotive-fast brain, and toned body, my next-door neighbor was enticing every single second of the day and every damn nanosecond of the night.

But I had mastered the fine art of restraint over the last year I'd spent on hiatus from any and every form of romantic relationship. And Nina never gave any indication that she was game for more. Even if she'd been game, I wasn't in the market for more than that, given the way my last relationship had imploded—with my ex behind bars.

With that kind of track record, I was taking a break from romance.

Friendship though? I knew what I was doing in that department, and I intended for Nina to stay there.

I banished the tempting thoughts of her once again.

I clicked open our text thread and asked her if I could extend my stay at Hotel Nina.

Her answer was swift, giving me the yes I'd been hoping for.

My day improved instantly. Definitely back to a B-plus. Setting the phone in its holder, I pulled out of the office lot and headed for my high-rise, calling Jake on the drive home. My attorney, who was also my good friend, answered on the first ring.

"If you keep calling me, I'm going to have to up my hourly. No more friendship discount for you," he said wryly.

A laugh burst from my chest. "If the rate you charge me is your friends-and-family discount, then I don't want to know what you charge your other clients," I said.

"Oh, yes, you do. You might switch to law if you knew what I was pulling."

"Doubtful. I like being the king of my domain too much," I said, since owning my production studio and taking all the risks—which meant reaping all the rewards—was what I liked. What I *loved*.

"With the contracts we just signed, I'd say you're the king, prince, and heir to your domain," Jake remarked. "Those were some epic deals."

"Exactly. That's why I'm calling, and this is a friend call so your hourly better be zero right now."

"What's that? I can't hear you."

"Drinks are on me. Can you hear me now?" I asked as I slowed to a stop at a red light.

"That was crystal clear," he deadpanned, but then cleared his throat. "Seriously though. Drinks are definitely on me, and yes, we need to celebrate inking deals for all these new shows. This weekend? You up for it?"

I put my foot to the gas when the light changed. "I'm always up for a night out."

"And will your pajama party friend be joining the festivities?" he asked in a high-pitched tone, clearly mocking me and, by extension, Nina.

I rolled my eyes. "Please. We don't have pajama parties. We have pillow fights. Get it right."

"Aww, that's so adorable. Do you two do face masks together and paint your nails too?"

"Of course, then we write in our diaries," I said, laughing. "Anyway, asshole, I'm sure Nina's up for a night out with the crew, but I'll ask her."

Jake took a beat then dropped the ribbing. "How are the sleepovers with her? That can't be easy."

As I turned on my street, I noodled on his comment briefly. Was I that transparent with my little bout of lust for her? No way. That wasn't possible. I'd never let on that I'd had a single stray dirty thought about her. I tossed back a question, deflecting. "Why do you say that?"

"Because you're you, and she's her, and you two have that weird mind meld going on half the time we're all together," he said, and I breathed a sigh of relief that nothing more was obvious to him.

"Just good friends. I still have the burn marks on my back from Rose. I'm not interested in anything right now," I said, telling the truth as I mentioned my ex. I didn't want to be involved with anyone, and Nina was the kind of girl who didn't do one-night stands. Plus, I didn't think Nina and I could ever be compatible in certain other ways. She was a good girl. And I was the type of guy who corrupted good girls.

"Which means you're keeping her warm at night with your sweet, charming personality? Got it," he said, returning to trash talk, like he often did.

"Sweet?" I asked with a scoff. "Sweet is for candy, and I don't care for candy. But charming? I'll take that as a compliment, thank you very much. And I'm spending the night again because the painters aren't done."

"Ah, yes, more proof that you're into her."

"Because I don't want to inhale fumes while I sleep?"

"You could have asked to crash at my place," Jake answered. "But you didn't. You're crashing with her."

"She's down the hall, and you're a mile away," I said, pointing out the obvious.

"A mile is not that far, and I'm not personally offended that you didn't ask. I'm just saying, actions speak louder than words, and yours say you have it bad for your neighbor."

But if actions spoke, so did inaction. I'd never pursued anything with Nina, and therefore I was in the clear. "No, my actions say I'm a wise man, choosing to keep my commute exactly the same."

"Yes, your commute. Of course." I could practically hear him roll his eyes.

"And on that sarcastic note, I definitely look forward to you buying all the drinks this weekend," I said, then we ended the call when I pulled into the building lot and headed for the elevator, shooting up to the tenth floor as I replied to the painter, letting him know that two more days was fine, but I hoped they'd be done no later. My parents were flying out next week and would be staying in the guest room.

When I reached Nina's door, I rapped twice. I didn't want to barge in on her. Growing up with sisters, you learned to knock on every door every time or else they'd put your head in a sling. I was bigger, taller, and stronger than my two sisters, but that didn't matter. There was nothing, no death ray, no tractor beam, no master ninja move stronger than the headlock administered by a sister who'd been walked in on.

But Nina didn't respond, so I took out the key and unlocked the door.

"Yoo-hoo. Honey, I'm home," I joked, calling out when I was inside.

It had become my regular greeting the last few nights. She'd usually respond with something like "I'm just grabbing the casserole from the oven" or "Let me take my curlers out."

But the walls echoed. She wasn't here.

She'd probably headed out for a quick errand or to grab an Earl Grey latte at her favorite shop down the street. The woman was addicted.

I dropped my keys on the entryway table, scanning her place, as had become my custom these last few days. It was so her, so feminine but not girly. Pillows in rich royal shades of purple and blue lined her couch, and framed photos of snowfalls, autumn leaves, and sun-drenched beaches hung on the walls. Her photos, since she snapped landscapes when she wasn't shooting bodies.

As I surveyed the scene, my eyes landed on a Post-it note on the fridge. *Adam, did you know that the heat shield for the Apollo missions could sustain temperatures of up to five thousand degrees Fahrenheit? Can you even imagine how hot that is?*

Smiling, I grabbed the note and folded it up, tucking it into my pocket. I opened the fridge, cracked open a beer, and scrolled through the Whole Foods app to place a dinner order for tonight, adding red, orange, and green peppers, along with carrots and chicken for the stir-fry I'd make.

As I hit send, my phone dinged with a new voicemail on my messenger app. It was from my buddy Brandon, who worked in Paris now. Ah, he must have snagged the number of a TV writer he'd been trying to track down for me, a hotshot who he thought might be perfect for one of the shows my company was helming.

I hit play as he rattled off his usual variation on a greeting—*"a stunning redhead walking down the street just stopped to give me her number"*—yes, his usual greetings were details of his alleged prowess with the French women.

I laughed because he was so full of shit. Well, he'd never had a problem with the ladies in college, but we both knew he wasn't trying to get strangers to stop, drop, and get on their knees for him. He was all talk. All facade. It was how he dealt with a past he wasn't over yet.

Someday I hoped he would be. Someday soon.

"Yeah, yeah, yeah," I muttered as I laughed. "Get to the good stuff."

He reeled off the screenwriter's name and number so quickly I blinked, missing most of it.

Grabbing a pen, I hunted around for a sheet of paper when I spotted one of Nina's ever-present notebooks. I crossed the distance to the kitchen counter to write down the number.

As I replayed the message, I flipped open the notebook to scratch down the digits, but the second I saw her writing on the page, the pen slipped from my fingers.

The voice on the message turned Charlie Brown–warbly.

My head swam with images.

What on earth was I looking at?

Was this what I thought it was?

This fantastic, delicious, filthy list.

In sweet, clever, brainy Nina's handwriting.

My friend.

My neighbor.

My deliciously depraved friend and neighbor.

I shouldn't have looked, but hell if I could tear my eyes away now.

4

ADAM

Arousal kicked in as soon as I read the first item on the list. When I reached the second, I was hard as a rock. And as I finished the third, I was sure I'd be imitating a skyscraper for days.

1. Get down on my knees.
2. Beg for it.
3. Talk dirty to me.

Scrubbing a hand over my jaw, I exhaled roughly.

This. List.

This filthy, fantastic list.

It didn't end there. More items filled the page, fantasy after filthy fantasy, elaborately detailed. Numbers four, five, six, seven, eight, and then nine.

Holy hell. The last few words of nine sent the

temperature in me skyrocketing. *F*ck me hard, f*ck me good, f*ck me for the first time.*

My eyes devoured them all, my body heating like a supernova. I was a spacecraft about to re-enter Earth's atmosphere, tearing through the atmosphere at five thousand degrees Fahrenheit or hotter.

Could I imagine it? Hell, yes. I was living it right now.

I shook my head, like I was trying to wake myself up in case this was a dream. The red-hot, dirty dream of discovering the girl-next-door's fantasies, all of them.

Except for one that wasn't finished. Number eleven —it looked like she'd started something with the word *watch* in it, but hadn't finished.

No matter. The rest was clear and explicit.

My skin sizzled as I read it again, my mouth watering at every item on this sexual bucket list.

Including number ten.

That one taunted me the most.

I tugged at my shirt collar.

Stepping away from the list, I paced around the kitchen. I was an explorer who'd stumbled across a precious artifact, one that had great and formidable powers.

My mind assembled the movie reel of her list, frame after debauched frame. Nina bent over the couch, ass in the air. Nina on her knees, her wrists tied behind her back. Nina begging, pleading, crying out for my shaft.

I flinched, surprised at the ruthless immediacy of the film in my head, the shamelessly erotic way I'd spliced together all the images to add me into the credits of her fantasy cast.

I was surprised, too, at the hammering of my pulse.

The rushing of my blood.

And the relentless desire her list stirred in me. This was more than simply being turned on by an idea.

I was turned on by the *idea of her*, in all these positions.

I swallowed roughly, turning around, walking back to the counter. I slammed the notebook shut, the illustrated owl on the front cover staring back at me with a grin across his feathered face. Like he knew something.

Like he was trying to tell me something.

What words of advice did the owl have for me?

I nearly smacked myself.

"Get it together," I muttered. "You're talking to an illustrated owl."

A wise man would have walked away. A wise man would pretend he'd never seen it and shove the list into the trunk in the back of his brain, locking it up and throwing away the key.

I'd thought I was a wise man. I'd vowed to become one after Rose pulled the wool over my trusting eyes, using me.

But right now, I didn't feel wise, and I didn't feel used.

I felt hungry.

Ravenous was more like it, and I wanted to devour my good friend.

Because according to this list, Nina—beautiful, sassy, captivating Nina—was a virgin.

A virgin with a naughty appetite.

And, it seemed, judging from number ten—*find the man to give me this list*—she was a virgin on an erotic mission.

I'd seen what happened to women who tangled with the wrong men. I'd witnessed far too much heartbreak from my sisters when they got involved with bad boys they hoped to turn into good guys. Never worked, never would.

The result was heartache and tears.

Some other man could find this list. Some other man could hurt my friend.

I couldn't let Nina give up her virginity—my God, what a beautiful, intoxicating gift—to some random guy she found online, or in a store, or at the freaking gym.

Number ten.

There was only one answer to number ten.

Me.

That man had to be me. I had to convince her that I was the one to give her all these fantasies, and that we'd come out on the other side the way we were right now —friends and neighbors.

But first, I'd start with food, with easy conversation, with the way we were. That was how I'd want her to see my proposition for my role in the list. To see that our friendship was the perfect basis for ten filthy commandments.

5

NINA

The shot was perfect.

Miss Sheridan down the hall had mastered the warrior pose.

She showed it to me one more time on her phone, nudging me, proud of her prowess. "See? How about that? I can't leave my twenty-two thousand, two hundred and one followers waiting. You are a doll for helping me shoot this video at last."

"I'm happy to do it. After all, I would never want to be the one to stand between you and even one of those twenty-two thousand, two hundred and one. They need to see your warrior pose," I said, completely serious, because this woman was a badass dame who simply needed a little tech support now and then. I was happy to provide it.

Miss Sheridan was a former showgirl and now she taught yoga classes both locally and on YouTube. She'd bought a new cell phone for the videos and had struggled to find the setting for horizontal—hence her *emergency* knock.

Boy, oh boy, did I know that struggle too.

"You should try my classes," she said, folding her hands together in a namaste. She still had the curves of a showgirl, and the attitude. "Yoga for Showgirls and Seniors is getting quite the following. And yoga is good for flexibility in the you-know-what."

I couldn't resist the bait. I raised an innocent eyebrow. "In the butt? Is that what you mean?"

Her jaw dropped, and she cackled. "And to think I was going to say it's good for flexibility in the bedroom."

I laughed. "I know. Just messing with you."

"Speaking of the bedroom, how are things with your roommate?" She wiggled her eyebrows, tipping her forehead toward the hallway.

"He's not my roomie. He's just using the guest room while his place is being painted."

She made an A-OK gesture with her fingers. "Right, sure," she said, in a way that made it clear she found my answer had holes like Swiss cheese in it.

"I swear he is," I said, insisting, because it was true. Adam and I were friends and only friends, and that was all I wanted.

My sole focus was on business and, as of an hour ago, finding a way to eradicate the overwhelming plethora of fantasies from invading my brain nonstop during work hours. Once I knew what my clients knew, I'd be able to connect with them on another level, like I wanted.

She hummed. "But he's a nice one. A sweet one. He fixed the door in my laundry room the other day. And just a few weeks ago, he hung some new shelves for me."

"He's a handy one too," I added, keeping it light.

"And so outgoing. He's like the sun. You can't tell me you don't feel chemistry with him." She arched a brow in question.

Her skepticism pierced me, and I looked away, my eyes landing on her tabby cat lounging in a streak of early evening sun cast through the window.

The cat stretched elegantly, looking like Evangeline, at ease in her body.

Something I was not, so I asked myself the questions Miss Sheridan was hinting at.

Did I feel chemistry with Adam? Smart, charming, easygoing Adam?

Friendly chemistry, for sure.

We were pals, birds of a feather.

And empirically, Adam was attractive. There were no two ways about that. With honey-brown hair, warm hazel eyes, a square jaw, and just the right amount of scruff, the man radiated magazine-quality looks. Like Scott Eastwood, with the same touch of rugged exterior.

But Adam was *good*.

And even though I was a virgin, I knew what I wanted.

A dark and dirty man to work through my wish list, the one that had been percolating in my head for years, fueled by the books I read, the videos I watched, the Tumblr feeds I devoured.

A rough man, a commanding man who'd help me cross off item after unholy item.

And all I needed from that unnamed man was to shed my virginity. To fulfill these rampant fantasies and eject them out of my head.

Adam was a straight-up kind of guy. I doubted he'd pin me down, shove my face into the pillow, and tell me to suck his—

I stopped the lust train, slapping on a smile for the older lady. "We are just friends," I told her, and that was the other reason I couldn't entertain romantic thoughts of Adam.

We'd become close friends over the last two years. He'd helped me grow my business, offering feedback on marketing and my online presence. His wisdom was so spot-on I'd become the most sought-after boudoir photographer in Sin City at age twenty-four.

As for him, I'd become his go-to friend, the one he played trivia games and shared podcasts with. That role had been easy to fill, especially after his last relationship turned sour, and he found his girlfriend not only using, but selling opiates near college campuses. She'd stolen money from him to fund her drug empire. To say Adam was jaded on romance was a euphemism.

He was turned all the way off love.

I headed for the door. "I'm glad your video is working now, and I can't wait to see your triangle pose," I told Miss Sheridan, and I left, walking down the hallway to my condo at the end.

When I opened the door, Adam stood in the kitchen

slicing peppers for dinner. He shot me his winning grin, the kind where his dimples shone.

That was my Adam. He was a good man, and seeing him here in my home warmed my heart.

* * *

I set down the fork, heaved a satisfied sigh, and gestured to the empty plates. "Fine, you win. My taste buds are definitely singing a rock anthem," I said, conceding.

"Excellent," he said, his hazel eyes twinkling. "Are we talking *'Don't Stop Believin''* or a *'For Those about to Rock, We Salute You'* kind of anthem?"

"Please. This is *'We Are the Champions'* level."

He rubbed his fingers on his shirt then blew on them. "Damn. That's tops. I impress myself."

I patted his shoulder. "Don't rest on your laurels though. One must always guard against complacency," I said, then lowered my voice to a whisper. "Or else—"

He held up a hand, shaking his head. "Don't say 'pumpkin.' Don't even say 'pumpkin.'"

"Pumpkin? What pumpkin? I was simply going to say you don't want to slip to *only a pop song* level of success for your dishes."

"Can't stoop to pop. I'm a rock-anthems-or-bust kind of man," he said.

"Don't I know it," I said as I picked up the dishes and brought them to the sink.

As we rinsed the plates and set them in the dishwasher, we caught up more on our workday. He told me about his two deals, and how excited he was for the shows to launch.

"I'm stoked about this new slate of shows. They're edgy and clever. The perfect dark comedies that today's viewers love."

"I can't wait to tune in when they're on," I said.

I loved his enthusiasm for his business. It matched my own for mine, and we'd always had that in common.

"And what about you? Did you capture some fantastic photos from your shoot?"

"I did," I said as we finished cleaning. "The couple that was in today—Marco and Evangeline—were great subjects. The camera loved them, and they seemed to enjoy their shoot too," I said.

"Of course they did. You're 'We Are the Champions' level good at your job."

"And on that high note, want to play a round of our favorite trivia questions game?" I asked as I folded the dish towel and set it back on the counter.

"With wine, of course?" he asked.

"Everything is better with wine," I answered, and we settled into the couch, glasses in hand. With each question, I was reminded once more of why I'd said to Miss Sheridan that we were just friends.

Because we were the kind of pals who teased and laughed, who poked fun and played games.

But then he grew quiet as we volleyed questions about new science facts at each other. Normally he'd make a joke about some impossible-to-answer question, pretend it was a trick by the game maker.

Only he didn't. He seemed lost in thought.

"Excuse me for a second," he said, and rose, heading for the guest room.

That's odd.

But ten seconds later, he returned, a determined look on his face as he sat next to me, closer than he had been.

I parted my lips to speak. "What's—?"

"Nina," he said, his voice rougher, deeper than I'd heard it before. "There's something I need to tell you."

Tension darted down my spine. Those words never preceded anything good.

What was he going to tell me? Was he leaving Vegas? I worried about that from time to time. He worked in the entertainment business, and his job could easily be moved to Georgia or Canada or Hollywood. While he traveled to those places a lot, Vegas was his home and his company's home. I hoped it would remain so, but you never knew. "Are you moving to Atlanta?" I blurted out.

He furrowed his brow. "What? No."

"Oh good. I was worried," I said, relaxing. But then, something else was bugging him. "What's going on?"

He scrubbed a hand across his jaw, exhaling, then meeting my gaze, his hazel eyes shining darker than usual, like there were secrets in them he was going to reveal. "I'm going to be blunt because I believe that's what you want. When I came home today, I needed to write a phone number down, and I flipped open your notebook. To grab a sheet of paper," he said, and my heart raced rabbit fast. My pulse sped off the charts.

"I wasn't prying, Nina, but I saw a list you'd written,"

he said, like he was laying out the facts he desperately
wanted me to believe.

A white sheet of shame descended over me. Mortifi-
cation took on a new meaning.

But inside my embarrassment something else
formed—a kernel of anger. Red and glowing.

"That was personal," I said, my jaw tight, as I moved
away from him. "You shouldn't have looked at it. You
shouldn't." Maybe if I said that enough, he'd forget what
he saw, erase it from his mind.

"I know I shouldn't have," he said, gravel in his voice.
"And I'd like to say I feel terrible for invading your
privacy. But . . ."

I furrowed my brow, confused. "You don't feel bad?
Then why are you telling me?"

He shook his head. "I wanted to feel bad, but I
couldn't find it in me to."

I shot him a stare. "Then why are you telling me?" I
asked again, more bite in my tone. I stood, heading to
the kitchen to clean the counter—anything to get away
from the embarrassment of my most private fantasies
revealed, right alongside my deepest secret.

His footsteps echoed across the floor, and in seconds
he moved behind me. "I'm telling you because of
number ten." His words rumbled across the air.

I knew what number ten was.

Number ten was the linchpin of the whole list.

Number ten would be the hardest item to
accomplish.

His body was inches from mine, so close I could
inhale his scent, like the winter woods, and a sliver of

desire thrummed in my veins, surprising the hell out of me.

The hairs on my neck stood on end. My mind went on high alert, racing through possibilities as quickly as I'd cycled through fantasies about Marco and Evangeline.

Was he about to say what I thought he was?

But Adam wasn't that kind of guy, I reminded myself.

I waited for him to speak next, to fill the pulsing silence, even though the noises in my head were so damn loud they nearly drowned out any words.

Adam dipped his face closer, brushing his mouth over my ear, and whispered, "Ask me, Nina. I'll be the man to do all those things to you for the first time."

He spoke in a command. Like me asking him was an instruction. No, it was an order.

He'd given me a command.

That shiver turned into a full-body shudder.

6

NINA

Adam was never in the cards.

For all the reasons I laid out in my head when Miss Sheridan had inquired. She wasn't the only one in my life who'd nudged me about Adam. My friend Lily had at her wedding, tugging me aside and asking when I was going to go for it. *Your wedding is making you loopy*, I'd teased. My friend Kate had simply arched a dubious brow.

Had they seen something in him I hadn't?

What would I see if I turned around?

Would I see sunshine, as I always saw with this man?

Or would I see midnight? Another side of Adam?

Part of me was terrified; another part was thrilled.

My mind raced through the myriad possibilities— what would happen to us if I asked him to bite me, have me, take me? Discover me on the bed and watch me touch myself? For once in my life, I wanted to be the one who was seen. I wanted to be watched. I craved the chance to say things like *watch me strip, watch me tease, watch me taunt.* Then I'd add, *Tie me up and make me take it hard.*

With Adam?

My pulse beat between my legs, the first sign.

But there were so many *what-ifs* to Adam as number ten.

We were frozen, poised on the edge of a building, staring down at the ground below, so far away. If we jumped, would there be a safe landing?

I licked my lips and pushed out words. It felt as if I were speaking for the first time. "What happens if I ask you?"

It was an open-ended question. He could answer it in many ways.

A low growl was his first reply, a dirty hum that sent a new wave of tingles all over me.

His mouth was dangerously close to my ear as he gave the rest of his answer. "Then I'd say yes. Then we'd work through your list. I'd fulfill all your filthy, fantastic dreams. You'd say no whenever you wanted. You'd set the rules, you'd set the boundaries, and I'd respect them," he said, and I trembled from the intensity of his words, the depth of his understanding. I shuddered, too, from his touch, because as he spoke, he slid a hand down my side, curling it over my hip. His touch was electric. Sparks thrummed through me.

"And what happens after I set the boundaries?" I asked, breathless and so eager, too, for more of his answers.

With a rasp I'd never heard from him before, he said, "Then I'll tell you to get on your knees and suck me so deep you feel it in the back of your throat. Or I'll bend you over the table and tie your wrists above your head so I can have my wicked way with your sweet pussy. So I can tease you and taunt you and deny your orgasms till I say you're good and ready to come."

A gust of breath escaped my lips. My knees wobbled. Those were my fantasies. Those were on my list. He'd read it, and he wasn't running. He was closing in on me, wanting. I could feel his desire. I could feel the heat radiating from his body.

Adam was turning me on in ways I'd never anticipated.

But dirty words weren't enough. Sharing desires wasn't sufficient either.

I needed to know we'd be okay. I needed to be certain we'd stay friends. That mattered more than this exquisite ache between my legs.

"But what happens to us?" I asked, while I longed to grab the counter, bend my body into an L, and beg him to yank down my jeans.

"What happens after dark, stays after dark," he said, a play on the city's famous motto. "Sex is sex, and friendship is friendship, and we call the shots. We set the ground rules. Here's mine: Consent comes first. You come second, third, fourth, and many more times. You come hard, you come relentlessly, you come when I say you come, you come again and again on my face, on my cock, on your toys, tied up, pushed down, with my fingers in you, however the hell you want. Then I come. Then we stay friends. How's that for ground rules?"

I quivered, and the ache between my legs turned into

a throb. A demanding, heavy throb that insisted on being answered.

Maybe Adam was in the cards.

Maybe he was *all* the cards.

"Promise we stay friends?" I asked, my voice feather-light and laced with burgeoning desire—desire I hadn't seen coming. Desire I'd never expected.

What was happening to me? Had Evangeline and Marco's passion unleashed a lust monster in me? Had Aphrodite done this? Sent my fantasies into overdrive with my best guy friend?

Adam.

Charming, clever, thoughtful Adam.

Adam was the guy next door.

But tonight, he was the man gripping my hip, digging his fingers hard into my flesh.

My cells cried out for his touch.

For his command.

And for his rough edge that I hadn't known existed.

He was showing it to me, just as I was revealing to him my secrets. He hadn't asked either—hadn't inquired why I was a virgin. It wasn't a state secret, but I didn't want to serve up my choices at this moment. I'd share that story with him another time.

"Damn straight we stay friends," he growled. "Isn't that what we were at dinner? Isn't that what we are all the time?"

"Yes. Yes, we are," I said with no reservations.

"And do you trust me?"

I blinked. "How can you ask me that? You have a key to my home. I trust you completely."

His shoulders relaxed. "Good. I always want to be the man you trust. And that's the kind of man you need for number ten."

"That is what I need." I took a beat, considering the enormity of the step we were taking. But then, everything made perfect sense. I didn't want a stranger. I didn't want a hookup. I wanted to feel safe as I explored. "So that's it? Those are the rules of engagement for my sex list?" I asked, because my logical brain liked to raise its hand at the most inopportune moments.

Like when Adam's thick erection pressed against my ass. The weight of his hard-on even through all these layers of clothing was intense.

"Those are the rules of engagement for your dirty, delicious, enticing, sexy-as-sin list. Unless you have any you want to add," he said, then rubbed the scruff of his jaw against my cheek.

My body screamed for contact. My mind loved the way he'd elaborated on my list, how he'd referred to it.

But there was one more rule to establish. "Protection," I whispered.

"I have condoms. We'll use them every time. No questions asked," he said, and I smiled privately.

I loved that he assumed I wasn't on protection already. If I were him, I'd assume that too. "I'm on protection and have been for years."

"You are?" His tone was laced with question. Understandably. But now was not the time to dive into why.

"Yes. If you're clean we don't have to use condoms," I said. "Are you? Have you been tested?"

His groan lasted for several carnal seconds. "I am. Clean bill of health at my last physical. I haven't been with anyone since."

I broke the hold he had on my hip. I spun around and took a few steps backward to the kitchen counter, feeling naughty, daring.

From a few feet away, I stared at my friend with new eyes, drinking in the cut of his jaw, the fire in his eyes, the expanse of his hard chest.

My eyes roamed over him. He was fully dressed, but fully revealed too. The outline of his arousal was visible through his pants. Thick and firm.

My mouth watered as I stared at the shape of it.

But tonight I wanted something else.

Something for me.

I didn't need to start at the beginning of my list. The first three items set the tone. I'd cross them off as I worked through the others.

I knew where to start.

"Okay, then. Now that we've tackled the rules of engagement, I'd like to try number four, please."

7

NINA

I wasn't ready for sex tonight.
  But I was primed and eager for touch.
  And for restraint.
  Aphrodite's advice rang in my ears.

Don't be afraid to be specific. Communication is key in any relationship, especially in an intimate one. Lay out your wishes. Speak your dreams. And hey, every now and then, you might want to present a detailed diagram or specific to-do list. There is nothing wrong with clarity. In fact, clarity can be incredibly sexy. Do you want your lover to bend you over the couch, bind your wrists, and kick your ankles apart? Then make it clear. Use your words, because words are as sensual as touch.

Yes. God yes. Those things, and more.

With a deep breath and a dose of goddess bravado, I parted my lips and said, "And here's how I want it."

Then I told him the basics of number four. "What do you think?" I asked, a touch of nerves in my voice.

His eyes seared me. "I think you're going to get everything you want. And everything you deserve, dirty girl."

A naughty smile tugged at my lips at the impromptu nickname. Lately, I'd felt like one, and like I'd needed to hide that side of myself. But the way Adam said those words made me feel like I could own the moniker at last. Like I could revel in it, rather than tuck it away, unseen.

He stalked over to me, closing the few feet between us, his eyes narrowed, shining with pent-up desire. Had that desire been there before or had I unleashed it in one night?

I didn't know. I wasn't sure if I wanted to know.

All I wanted was number four.

But before he followed my detailed instructions, he clasped my cheek. "I'm going to give you all that you want, but there's something I need to do before I turn you around and fuck you with my fingers."

I shivered with anticipation. "What is it, Adam?"

His eyes blazed with lust as he brushed his finger across my top lip. "Kiss those luscious, sexy, pouty lips."

My eyes widened. *Yes.* I nodded, took off my glasses, and in less than a second, his lips were on mine.

He didn't prime me. Didn't kiss me gently.

Instead, he *took*.

He seized the kiss, his lips consuming mine in the

span of a heartbeat. With one hand on my cheek, another on my hip, he pushed me back against the counter and held me in place, devouring my mouth.

I'd never been kissed like this.

The others before Adam, and there weren't many, were soft and sweet.

They kissed like they were testing the terrain.

Adam was not tentative. He was resolute.

And this kind of kiss was so foreign, I wasn't sure what to do with my hands, my body. I stood rigid, even as my insides melted.

Was I supposed to touch him too? To run my hands up and down his chest? I had no idea, so I tried to focus on his moves, as if the camera of my mind was recording them to replay later.

He barely used his tongue. He was all lips and heat and strength, and absolute control. He slid his thumb to my jaw, his fingers to my chin, and yanked my head back. Kissing me harder. Making everything clear. He owned this moment, and he owned me.

My neck was exposed, my kisses were his as he whispered, "Do you need to be kissed like a dirty girl?"

That was when I relaxed fully. That was when I turned to liquid. I knew what to do with my body. *Give in.*

All of me melted.

"Yes," I whispered.

"Dirty girls get kissed like this," he said, tilting my head and licking a line across my lips.

Holy hell.

He was showing me how he'd kiss me in other ways.

At the corner of my lips, he flicked his tongue. Then he drew a long, lingering line across my lips again, murmuring as he went, like he was going down on me. When he stopped, his eyes blazed with desire. "You taste so damn good, and I bet you're going to taste even better when you show me how much you like coming on my face."

Electricity shot across my skin, traveling up and down my body. "I bet I will," I said, feeling emboldened.

Something like a growl seemed to rumble up his chest as he shook his head. "But not tonight. You know why?"

"Why?" I asked, nerves and desire thrumming through me.

He dipped his face near mine. "Because I know how you want number five. I know how you want me to eat you out. You're going to get number five when you show me how good you can beg for my mouth, like the dirty girl you are. You're going to have to plead before I bury my face between your legs."

Flames licked across my body. I was an inferno, and he was my oxygen. I wanted him to fan the flames of my fire. "Do I have to beg you tonight?" I asked, and the possibility thrilled me.

He brushed his thumb along my chin. "No. Not tonight. We'll get to that. But you will do as I say right now. Is that clear?"

I nodded, pleasure tripping through me, making me wetter.

He issued a command, saying, "Answer me with words, Nina."

I gulped. "Yes. I understand."

"Good," he said, absently running his hand over the outline of his erection. *So hot.* "Tell me something."

"Yes?"

He lifted his chin, his eyes roaming over me, lingering on my breasts. I glanced down, took in my erect nipples poking through the soft fabric of my shirt. I arched my back, the material straining further as he asked, "Are you wet from the way I kissed you?"

I nodded. "So wet."

"Are you aching for me to touch you?"

Oh God. I wasn't going to last long. "So ready," I said, breathless.

"Good. Now turn around and put your hands on the counter."

Swiveling around, I did as I was told, gripping the edge. His hands were fast, practiced.

Unbuttoning my jeans, unzipping, sliding them down my hips. He was exposing me, and my muscles tightened. I wasn't ashamed of my body. Not in the least. But with each inch he revealed, I was keenly aware that my friend was seeing me in a new way, just like he'd seen inside my mind when he read the list. Now he'd be seeing my body fully. All my skin, all my flesh.

No one had.

No man had ever taken my clothes off before.

In seconds, my jeans hit my calves, and I tried to step out of them. "No," he growled. "Leave them right there."

He kicked the inside of my right ankle, then my left, spreading me as far as I could go with my jeans pooled at my legs. *Like a restraint.* Like I had imagined.

He rose, humming. "Your ass. Your fantastic ass. I bet it's as luscious as I've imagined it was so many damn times," he said, cupping my cheeks over my panties.

Reality slammed into me. He'd thought about my bare ass before? And I had the answer to the question I'd asked myself moments ago—*had that desire been there before or had I unleashed it in one night?*

This wasn't the first time he'd thought about me like this. I wasn't a new notion to him, and quite possibly he'd been craving me for some time.

My head didn't know what to make of this new intel, but my body did—my skin sizzled. My heart slammed harder against my chest, an insistent, demanding rhythm of lust and longing.

Adam wanted me, had wanted me for a while, and I liked his desire.

I liked everything he was doing to me tonight too.

He slid my panties down to my ankles, leaving them there with my jeans. And leaving me half-naked before him in my kitchen. Exposed, wet, needy.

And waiting.

8

ADAM

There were beautiful sights.

A snow-capped mountain in the Pacific Northwest.

A waterfall in Hawaii.

A cobblestoned street in Paris.

And then there was Nina Bellamy—smooth white skin; toned, supple legs; and the most fantastic ass I'd ever seen.

Those cheeks.

I wanted to bite them. To leave teeth marks on her flesh.

Twin globes of squeezable, kneadable, absolutely spankable flesh. And I had to get my hands on every inch of her body that was begging for my touch. She raised her ass, offering herself to me, and hell, did I ever need her.

But first, I had to give the woman what she wanted.

Her list was branded on my brain, so I took off my belt slowly, loop by loop, letting her hear the slap of the leather against my palm as I removed it. "You want it like this, dirty girl," I rumbled.

"Yes, yes, I do."

"And you're going to get what you want."

With my belt removed, I curled my body over hers, my chest to her back, my hands reaching for her forearms, pulling them closer. She arched against me, seeking contact. "Such a greedy girl. Is it hard for you to wait?" I asked as I wrapped the belt around her wrists.

"So hard."

"I bet you're soaked. I bet you're aching for my fingers. I bet you'd beg for my cock right now."

"Oh God. Yes. I would. Do you want me to?"

It was a desperate cry from her, and I hated denying it. But we'd get there. "Well, you can't have that tonight. Dirty girls need to wait," I told her as I fastened the belt around her soft hands. Then I tightened it one more notch, and she let out a wild moan, chased by a question. "What can I have tonight?"

"If you show me how much you want my fingers, I'll give you everything you need. But you have to show me, Nina. Show me how badly you're aching for me."

She stretched her arms across the counter, bending her back into a flat line, lifting her ass even higher. She turned her face to me, the good student eager to please her teacher. "Is this good?"

I gazed at her glistening sex.

She was bare, ready, and so goddamn beautiful.

Pink, virginal, pure.

And, according to her list, I was going to be the first one to touch her.

What a gift.

What a heady gift.

I'd take my sweet time opening this gift as I gave her the fantasy she craved—bound, exposed, fingered from behind.

My hands curled around her succulent ass, and she moaned, a delicious, needy sound.

I squeezed her flesh, savoring the feel of her in my palms.

She wriggled against me, her body making it damn clear that she liked it. That she wanted more.

That she needed to be touched, stroked, taken.

I planned to give it all to her, but first I had to go off script. For her, and for me. Because I wanted something desperately. As I kneeled behind her, she gasped, turning to look at me. Her eyes were wide and innocent.

Etched with filthy curiosity.

"I'm going to give you number four, but I need just a taste of you first," I said, then licked a tantalizing line across her ass. *Right there.* That tempting crease where her ass met the top of her thigh. That absolutely intoxicating location on the map of a woman's body. I traveled across it, flicking my tongue along that boundary.

She tasted so sweet, her skin smelling faintly of cherries. *Of course.* Cherries are sexy. They're lipstick red. Lingerie red.

"Oh God," she whispered.

I lavished the same attention on her other cheek, inhaling the scent of her arousal. Salty and sexy.

I couldn't wait to taste her.

I rose and dipped my hand between her legs.

She gasped, then pressed her lips together, like she was holding in sounds.

I slid one finger across the most slippery, perfect flesh I'd ever felt. She shivered, but still stayed quiet.

That wouldn't do. I had to help her through her nerves.

I dropped the dirty, rough tone I'd been using. "Nina, are you afraid to make a sound?"

"I don't know," she whispered, sounding fearful. "I've never done this. Except in my head."

I bent over Nina, pressed my cheek to hers, gentle in my question. "Do you want me to stop?"

"God, no. It's just . . ."

"Just what, baby?"

She squeezed her eyes shut, shuddering, but not from pleasure—from worry. "Adam . . . what if I'm too loud? What if the sounds I make are ridiculous?"

I chuckled softly and kissed her cheek. "I assure you, Nina, the sounds you make are going to be so goddamn sexy, they'll only make me harder. Want to know how I know?"

"Yes," she said softly, her body relaxing again.

I reached for her bound wrists, raised her arms, and spun her around. Guiding her hands to my jeans, I rubbed her palms over the outline of my erection. "Believe me now?"

She was quiet at first, her expression hard to read. Then her lips curved into a naughty grin. "I believe you, and I believe in your eight inches."

I shook my head in admiration. "You naughty, sexy

woman. Now let's get you back where you belong." I returned her to the position she'd been in, still me, still in my regular voice. "Tell me what you want. Do you want to scream? Do you want to moan? Do you want to cry out?"

"I do," she said in a whisper. "I want all that."

She was ready now; she had the reassurance. Rough again, husky again, I gave her a command. "Then *do it*. I want all your sounds, all your pleasure, all your ecstasy," I said, then slid one arm up her body and into her hair. Gripping her gorgeous locks, I tugged, and she moaned instantly. "That's right, dirty girl." I pressed the outline of my erection against her bare ass, letting her feel what she did to me. "Your noises *only* arouse me. They *only* make me harder. Give them to me. Give them to me right now."

Another needy moan was my reward.

My erection twitched, begging to be set free.

Not tonight.

Tonight was for her.

And for all her glorious wetness. With her ankles spread as far as they could go, I slid my other hand back between her legs.

I stroked, getting her ready, prepping her. The woman was so turned on, my fingers were coated in her in seconds as I played with her decadent center, sliding my fingertips between her lips, then rubbing that gorgeous swell. So hard, so insanely aroused.

She was a dream.

And my job was to deliver on *her* dream.

Part of me knew I should take her tenderly and go

softly because this was all new to her. But another part knew I had to respect the woman's wishes.

She didn't want tender.

She'd made that damn clear.

But I was determined not to hurt her. I had to find the balance she might not even realize she needed. Had to help her feel safe, respected, before I pushed in the way she wanted.

I tested her first, dipping one finger inside.

So warm.

I tugged on her hair, pressed my lips to her neck, and whispered hotly, "Fuck my finger, dirty girl. Show me you want it."

"I do. God, I want it so much," she said, rocking back against me fast, furiously.

Yes, this was good. This was how she'd get ready. On her terms. Using my finger to get her sweet heat ready for more.

After a few minutes, I was sure Nina could handle it.

And I bet she'd been taking it hard and good with vibrators for years. I bet she had drawerfuls of them, and I was confident, too, that she'd tell me all about her dirty little collection. That it was on the tip of her tongue, just waiting to be set free. I could do that for her. I could be the one she shared it all with. I was her safety zone for every after-dark thought. "Tell me something."

"I'll tell you anything," she said, and I grinned. Yep, Nina wanted to be unlocked.

I had the key. I kept turning it. "Do you fuck yourself

with toys, dirty girl?" I moved my finger faster, stroking her clit with another one.

"Yes. I did that last night."

Lust tore through me like wildfire. The images flashed in front of my eyes. The awareness of what she'd done while I slept nearby. "When I was in the guest room, you were pleasuring yourself with a toy?"

"Yes. I used my rabbit. I like it hard and deep. So deep."

Enough said.

She was good to go.

My virgin could handle what I had in store for her. I lowered my mouth to her neck, kissing her possessively as I added another finger, lust rocketing through every molecule in my body. "Were you on your back last night? Your legs spread nice and wide?" I asked as I thrust a third finger into her hot, tight center.

"No. I was on all fours."

I nearly lost it. She masturbated on her hands and knees. Forget five thousand degrees. I was hotter. "I'm going to need to see that. Need to watch you do that. I'm going to watch you and come all over your beautiful back when you do that."

She pulsed around my fingers, quivering, turning even wetter, even slicker. "Yes, do that. Watch me. Watch me and come on me. Come all over me," she said, and her voice wasn't her own. It was sensual and smoky while she chased her pleasure, pumping her pelvis against my fingers as I stroked her just as hard.

Just as ruthlessly.

Just the way she wanted it.

She was no longer nervous, no longer scared.

She was all in, and I was so damn glad she'd found her freedom.

We were perfectly in sync as I stroked, rubbing her clit, twisting my fingers in and out, searching and finding that spot—that wonderful X-marks-the-spot of euphoric pleasure.

"Yes, oh God, yes. I need to come. Please let me come.

Please, please, please."

This woman. My God. She knew what she wanted. Knew what she had to have.

Her entire body shook as I tugged her hair and stroked her sweet center. "Ask me one more time," I growled. "Ask like a good dirty girl."

She moaned to the heavens. "Adam, please let me come. I'm begging you."

I nipped her neck, my voice ragged against her skin. "Come all over my hand. Come like the good little virgin you are. Give it all to me."

And she did.

Holy hell, she did.

She shuddered, and a wave of pleasure seemed to roll over her. And again, and again, and again.

Her lips parted in the most magnificent O as she cried out. Her sounds reached the ceiling. They reverberated throughout her home. They rang in my ears like the most gorgeous song I'd ever heard.

It was as if she'd never come before. Not like this. Not this hard. Not this intensely.

And I suspected she hadn't.

When she came down minutes later, her eyes were glossy, her expression hazy. But she smiled then nibbled on her lip. I felt like a king.

That look on her face did something to my chest, like my heart was squeezing. I'd done that to her. I'd made her feel something she'd longed for. My friend. My wonderful, daring friend who'd trusted me with her most secret self.

"Did you like that, dirty girl?" I asked, my tone a little softer now, just me again.

She smiled, like she was still buzzed. "I loved it. I've never felt anything like that before." Then her shyness returned. An innocent little look as she cast her eyes down then back up. "Adam, that was my first. No one else has made me come but me."

My chest glowed from that knowledge, and I liked it so much, probably more than I should have. I kissed her cheek, this time softly, but I couldn't stop savoring the depth of this first.

I was the lucky recipient of Nina's first climax with another person.

It was heady, a rush of both pleasure and something else too.

Something a little deeper.

Something I didn't expect to feel.

Possession.

But I couldn't linger on these unexpected feelings in my heart, because another organ had more pressing needs.

And so did Nina, who lifted her chin and asked,

"Can I touch you now? Can I do the same to you? It's number six, after all. *Touching a man.*"

A shudder racked my body, but it wasn't just from my hedonistic side. Of course I wanted her to touch me. I wanted her hands all over my length, then her lips, her tongue, and her whole luscious mouth.

But it was the way she asked that nearly wrecked me. So sweet, so desperate. That sound did something to me. Hooked into me in a way that seemed dangerous. The more I let her take the reins, the greater the chance this exploration would become a give and take. And if it did, it would no longer be about her list. It'd become something else. And something else might be too risky.

We'd set rules for a reason; we'd erected boundaries because we had to.

I had to honor them. And part of honoring them was keeping the focus on her. Her list included touching a man for the first time, but it sure as hell didn't include a handjob. It did, however, explicitly detail something else involving hands. *My hand.* I was a diligent teacher, and I planned to give my student what she'd asked for.

I ran a finger across her soft cheek. "Yes. You can touch me. And then we'll do number seven. You can watch me jack myself till I come on your lips."

Call it the *number seven special.*

Her brown eyes lit up with desire. "Yes."

A minute later, I'd untied her hands, pulled up her pants, and unzipped my jeans. I freed my length from the confines of my boxer briefs.

She licked her lips when she saw my dick for the

first time. I gripped my shaft, stroking it once, long and lingering, watching her eyes turn hazier with lust.

When I reached the tip, I said, "Get on your knees."

She dropped to the floor.

"Give me your right hand."

She lifted it, offering it to me. I took her hand, wrapping mine over hers as I brought her soft palm to my shaft. The second she touched me, her whole body seemed to melt. She pressed her lips together, like she was holding in some kind of sound of wonder, like she'd stepped outside after a winter's worth of snow and experienced sunshine. Like she was soaking in warmth for the first time in ages.

"*Adam,*" she said in a heady whisper, her eyes wide.

I could feel my control slipping with the way she said my name. I had to remember who we were—in this moment, she couldn't be Nina, my good friend. She was the woman who wanted to know how it felt to be dirty for the first time.

And dirty girls needed instructions from their teachers.

"Grip me harder," I ordered.

She circled her hand tighter, making a fist, and a groan worked its way up my chest. To be touched like this, by someone taking her first trip to this country was so intense, so much sexier than I'd ever expected.

A wave of pleasure crashed over me as Nina caressed my throbbing length, stroking up and down. "You're so hard, and the skin is so soft," she said, whispering like she was in church.

The moment felt that way. *Reverent.*

But unholy, too, because of what I was about to do to her. The angels would look the other way and shield their eyes when they saw what was coming.

"One more stroke, dirty girl. That's all you get," I said.

"But you feel so good," she pleaded, staring at my length, then looking into my eyes as she touched me, sending red-hot sparks through my body. "I love it," she whispered under her breath, like she was confessing a secret.

My erection twitched in her hand because, hell, I loved it too.

Too much.

"That's enough," I said crisply. "Time for number seven. Just the way you want it. Put your hands behind your back, and watch me. Don't take your eyes off me."

"I won't."

With her like that, on her knees, gazing at me, I stroked my shaft, grateful for the relief. I was so wound up, so turned on from her coming, from her touching me, that it wouldn't take long. But I needed a little something.

"Get my dick wet with your juices. Make it easier for me to jack off in front of you, like you want."

Thrusting her hand inside her jeans and between her legs, she coated her fingers in the evidence of her climax. She reached for my erection, then spread her wetness along my length. The look in her irises as she touched me was one of wild thrill.

"Good. Now watch me. Don't close your eyes at all."

She wrapped her arms behind her back and didn't look away.

With my fist curled tight, I stroked hard, fast, rough. Long thrusts and jerks as all the pent-up pleasure tore through me like a tsunami, taking me to the edge in mere minutes.

"Open your lips, sweet girl."

She took orders like she took pictures. With precision and focus and passion. Her lips parted, and she waited for me to come on her lips.

My orgasm ripped through me, and I gave it all to her.

My greedy girl lapped me up like I was dessert, like she was famished and she intended to finish every last drop on her lips.

I shuddered, the aftershocks rocking through me in a blast of white-hot pleasure.

When I settled, I pulled up my jeans and told her to stay put, my voice softer now. "I'll be right back, baby. I'm going to clean those gorgeous lips of yours."

Shortly I returned from the guest room with a wet washcloth, wiped the come off her chin, then washed my hands. I set the cloth on the counter, making a mental note to toss it in the wash later. *Obviously.*

I reached for her, and she rose, those eyes wide and curious as she asked, "Was that good for you?"

I sighed happily, but sadly too. How could she think this night was anything but perfect?

I clasped her cheeks, speaking the full truth. "Tonight was in another realm. And there's more where that came from."

She shot me a small smile, still a little nervous, but a little eager too. "Good. I want more."

"I'll give you everything you want," I said, and then I took something I wanted.

I wanted a good night kiss.

A tender kiss.

This time I was soft and gentle. She seemed to like it, trembling in my arms.

Trouble was, I liked it too.

I liked it beyond the boundaries of our deal.

Outside the rules.

I liked it because it was her. Her sweetness, her loveliness. Her soft kiss made my chest ache. It was full of everything that made this woman my close friend—trust and compatibility.

And that was dangerous for the rules of our engagement.

Time to shove all these unwarranted emotions out of my head.

I scooped her up, took her to her room, and set her on the bed. I tucked a finger under her chin. "I'll see you in the morning, and I'll make your favorite breakfast," I said, because that would reset us. That was what we did. I cooked for her, and we talked about anything and everything.

That was us—our friendship.

And I needed to recalibrate.

She lifted her chin and looked at me sweetly, so damn sweetly. "Good night, Adam."

"Good night, Nina," I said, fighting the wish to stay.

I went to my bed, stripped to nothing, and slid under

the covers. I rated this night an A, but even with top marks, sleep didn't come easily. My brain whirred with too many thoughts. Thoughts and ideas I was wildly unprepared for.

But I still had questions. Or rather, I had one. In the morning, though, I'd ask her.

9

NINA

Even the shower felt new.

The hot water streaming over my skin was a fresh sensation.

Like I was feeling it for the first time.

I raised my face to the spray, letting it cascade over my cheeks, my shoulders, my belly.

The water traveled down my skin, like it was forging a new path over a new person.

This was crazy.

I was still me. Still irreverent, passionate, introspective me, the woman who loved watching the world go by through her lens, the person who craved facts and information, the friend who was there in a heartbeat when needed.

I was still that woman, wasn't I? I was still a businessperson, a neighbor, a friend.

But I was someone else now too.

Someone who *knew*.

Someone who knew sensations, desires, firsthand, with another person.

I didn't know much. I barely knew a few things about the way bodies tangled together, and how touch could turn to more.

But I'd started to explore that land. I'd pushed open the door to a secret club last night and sneaked inside. The club of mutual pleasure.

I'd been giving myself orgasms for years. The landscape of my nightstand bureau was mapped with mountains of vibrators, hills of batteries, and valleys of late-night fantasies. My Amazon account was privy to my personal habits—how many toys I obtained every year, how frequently I replaced them. I had quite the impressive collection.

But none of my toys had given me what Adam gave me.

Freedom from my own hands.

Freedom to let go. To surrender to another's touch. To the things I'd craved most.

Adam gave me the chance to give in to pleasure, to turn the keys over to another person. And it was wondrous.

As I remembered his filthy words, his firm commands, and his adherence to my written wishes, a hot shiver raced through me, but it was chased by something else.

By a quick burst of unexpected emotion. My throat tightened, and I was entirely unsure where this feeling was coming from. A feeling of something like . . . gratitude? Was that it? Was I simply grateful that Adam had administered my first non-solo O?

As I spread cherry body wash over my legs, I shook my head, the answer to my question coming quickly.

No, it wasn't gratitude. It was something stronger.

This kernel inside me felt closer to hope, too much like a wish for something beyond the bedroom.

That was a problem.

That wasn't what last night was about.

Hell, that wasn't what my list was about.

My list was a road map to and through pleasure, and only pleasure. It was a chance for me to learn a new language, one that had been impossible to speak when I was with clients, having private conversations. And it was my opportunity once and for all to move beyond my mind. To take all the desires in my head and explore them so they'd stop gnawing at me.

I rinsed my body, turned off the shower, and dressed, listening to another episode of *Ask Aphrodite*. A listener had wanted to know the hostess's best advice when it came to communicating with a lover. Turned out to be the perfect wisdom for me too.

After drying my hair and applying blush and mascara, I turned off the podcast and took a deep breath, ready to face Adam in the bright light of morning.

Adam, my friend.

Adam, my neighbor.

And Adam, my very temporary lover.

That was all, although we weren't done with that role. We had more erotic hills to climb, and I hoped we'd summit them without more of these pesky morning-after questions.

Still, would everything be different for us in the light of day? Could we still be us?

I wasn't sure, but I had to try, and that required more honesty. We'd always been honest and open as friends, so nothing should change now that we were temporary lovers. We'd stay honest, and that meant the question of *why* would need to be answered sooner rather than later.

Surely he was curious. I'd be curious too if I were him. Rather than waiting for him to ask, I chose to tackle it head-on, recalling Aphrodite's most recent words.

The key to communication is facing your fear. Why are you afraid of what your lover might say when you reveal yourself? Ask what scares you. Are you afraid he or she will judge you? Will look at you differently? These are normal worries, but facing them is brave, and moving past them can give you the keys to your future. So let me leave you with this: Don't be afraid to speak your mind. Talking is sexy. Sharing is sensual. You don't have to reveal everything, but intimacy comes from honesty, and when you can speak truthfully, you just might find yourself reaching new levels of connection.

I wasn't sure it was intimacy I sought so much as knowledge. But both went down the same path. The path of truth.

With my shoulders squared, I left my bedroom, resolute that we'd be the same and I'd talk to him as I always had.

Once I entered the living room, my nose lifted and I inhaled the most fantastic scents.

Breakfast. Adam's omelets. Fresh mushrooms and eggs and slices of avocado. And coffee. The rich aroma of a cup of morning joe.

It was heaven.

My mouth watered as I turned into the kitchen to find him at the stove. He wore only jeans as he cooked.

I blinked.

Why wasn't *this* on my list? This was a fantasy I hadn't known I had. This handsome man shirtless and making food for me.

I stared at the lean muscles of his back, his toned biceps, and his sinewy forearms as he folded the eggs, singing under his breath.

He flipped the omelet then brought the spatula to his mouth, crooning softly about being hooked on a feeling.

A smile took over my face. That song.

I loved that song.

Loved even more that Adam was himself the next day. Singing in the kitchen.

"I can't believe . . ." I sang softly, offering the next line in the tune.

He spun around, but his frown of confusion quickly turned into a grin as he handed me a second spatula. "Duet?"

"But of course."

I joined in, singing in harmony about lips as sweet as

candy. We cruised through the song, hitting some notes, missing others. And as we reached the lyrics about good love, I told myself it was just a song. They were just lines. We were having a blast.

And it was everything I wanted as he finished making our breakfast while we rocked out karaoke-style in my kitchen.

Talk about *not weird*.

The sheer normalcy of it lubricated the path to my admission. As soon as we sat down to eat, I jumped off another cliff.

10

NINA

"It's because of my sister," I said.

He tilted his head, his eyes waiting for me to say more. "Ella?"

"Yes. She's a single mom. As you know."

"I do," he said, then took a bite of the mushroom omelet.

I took a bite too, chewed, then spoke again. "And don't get me wrong. Her son is the coolest eleven-year-old I know, but . . ." I heaved a sigh. "She had him when she was seventeen."

He nodded. "Right. I sort of did the math the few times we've visited her," he said, since he'd met my sister and her kid, and my parents too. They lived nearby.

"She didn't plan on getting pregnant in high school, but she wasn't going to give up the baby. It wasn't easy," I said heavily, remembering the terror on Ella's face when she'd learned she was having a baby. "I was only in eighth grade. We'd always been close, and I wanted desperately to help her, to fix the problem. But there was, of course, nothing to be done. My parents didn't want her to have an abortion, and she didn't either. She'd planned to give up the baby for adoption."

"That must have been tough for Ella." His eyes filled with sadness.

"But once she was further along, she couldn't go through with the adoption," I said, recalling Ella's tears, her heartache. "I used to hear her crying at night, and in the morning, she'd talk to my mom about what to do."

"That's so hard. I can't even imagine how my sisters would have handled that," he said sympathetically, his eyes soft as they locked with mine.

"My parents supported her choice. They understood it too—why she'd had a change of heart. But once he was born, everything was upended for her, and for them too. They became grandparents, and, in a way, parents again."

"It's the kind of life change that shocks everyone," he said, taking a second to squeeze my arm, a friendly, caring squeeze.

"And she also took it upon herself to make sure I wouldn't follow in her footsteps. She urged me to be careful, to use protection. It was nonstop, her advice train. And, of course, it was and is good advice," I said, and took a drink of the coffee, thinking of my overprotective sister. "Her advice worked. But in a different way."

He lifted a curious brow, as he took a bite of the omelet. "How so?"

"I made a different decision then—to wait. I didn't

want to take a single chance, Adam. I didn't want that type of soul-ripping, bone-crushing heartache. And I also knew from an early age what I wanted in life."

"Your photography," he said, smiling, like he was delighted to know the answer.

I smiled too. "I knew what I wanted when I was thirteen and my parents gave me my first camera. All I ever wanted was to be a photographer. To go to art school, to learn the craft. I didn't want anything to derail my plans. And when Ella got pregnant, I learned exactly how one mistake, one stolen moment where you took a risk, could backfire. Could capsize your future. Even though my parents helped, Ella had to drop out of high school for the first six months after the baby was born. My mom cut back at her job to help with the baby. And when Ella finally went to college, it took her six years and so many sleepless nights to get her degree."

"That's rough," he said, shaking his head and reaching for my hand, clasping it. "I had no idea how hard it was for her."

"She's on the other side now. An amazing nurse, with a great kid. Her own place too. But it took a long time, Adam," I said, squeezing his hand in return. "And I wanted something different. I wanted my dreams first, and my dreams meant a bachelor's degree. I promised myself I would remain a virgin all through college. But I wasn't stupid. I took precautions just in case. I started on protection back then, because I didn't want to ever worry about a broken condom. I knew I had to be in charge of my own fate and my own body. And I suppose I figured I'd meet someone after college, but I haven't met anyone I liked enough," I said with a *what can you do* shrug. "And honestly, it was easier to devote all my energy to work and photography."

He flashed a proud grin, gesturing around my home and to the studio at the far end of the hallway where I shot my pictures. "And it paid off. You're so young and so far ahead in your career, and you own your own home at twenty-four. That's amazing."

"Thank you," I said, and I was proud too—I'd accomplished a lot already at my age, and I was relentless with my drive. I'd shut most things out of my life except for friends and photography for the last few years, dating only sparsely. "And I'm glad of that. Even when I dated, I never met anyone who thrilled me."

He scoffed. "Because you dated tools." He took another bite of his breakfast.

"Gee, thanks."

He set down his fork, leveling me with an honest stare. "Well, they kind of were, Nina. That guy Kenny? He was a professional poker player, and all he talked about were different combinations of cards. He nearly put me to sleep the night we all went to dinner. Wait, I think he did. If memory serves, I fell asleep at the table."

I didn't want to laugh, to admit I'd had bad taste, but I couldn't help myself. "So he wasn't terribly scintillating."

"'Scintillating'? He was tedious."

With a huff, I shrugged. My admission. "Okay, he was duller than Dullsville."

"Good. While we're at it, how about Jared? Wasn't he, like, a product manager of spreadsheets, or something equally mind-numbing? You'd need a microscope to find his sense of humor."

My lips quirked into a grin, as I tried to rein in a chuckle. "No. The requirement was actually the world's strongest microscope to find it," I said, then laughed. It was so good to be normal with him the next day. To poke fun at me, together. To be who we'd always been with each other. He'd seen me half-naked, he'd sent me soaring to the heavens, and he'd come on me, then watched me lick his release off my lips. And still, we were laughing and teasing the next morning. It was so easy to be with him. To be us, and this conversation tugged at the part of my brain that craved interesting facts. "Are you thinking what I'm thinking? What *is* the world's most powerful microscope?"

Like twin gunslingers, we grabbed our phones from our pocket holsters, fingers swiping. I beat him to the punch.

"Berkeley has a twenty-seven-million-dollar electron microscope," I blurted out.

"It lets you see to a resolution that's half the freaking width of a hydrogen atom," he said, jumping in.

"That's one ten-millionth of a millimeter," I said, my jaw dropping with wonder. "It can see everything."

He smiled as he read more, devouring intel about microscopes, then he stopped and met my gaze. "Look at us," he said, kind of amazed.

My heart skittered knowing we were on the same wavelength. "Yeah, look at us."

"We're doing this. Like we said we would last night.

Breakfast, and lightning-fast searches to look stuff up, and talking."

"We're us," I said, seconding him, then I returned to the previous topic, because digging into my reasons, my choices, felt good. "Adam?"

"Yeah?"

"Maybe I wasn't so great at picking men. Maybe I was drawn to guys I didn't have a great connection with because I knew what I wanted in bed."

His brow knitted. "I'm not following, but keep going, because I want to."

I swallowed, drawing a deep breath of air. "I think I always knew what I wanted in bed, and that it would be hard to find it, and harder still to voice it. So I chose the other path—where I wouldn't ever be faced with voicing my desires. I chose men who were unlikely to stimulate my mind, and so I kept my desires locked up."

His expression turned serious. "Why is it hard to speak about what you want?"

My throat tightened, but I pushed past the fear, like Aphrodite urged me to do. "Because I might be a virgin, but I don't want sweet and tender sex. And it's hard to say that. Because society expects virgins to want sex a certain way."

He set down his fork, studied me intensely. "There is nothing wrong with what you want. There is nothing wrong with kinky desires. I think it's sexy and smart and hot as hell to write down all those fantasies."

I sighed, relieved. "Sometimes I feel like a huge pervert. Like, when I'm with my clients, I sometimes picture them sleeping together afterward and imagine the things they'd do, the things I'd orchestrate. Doesn't that make me a pervert?"

"No. Your job is sexy. It's sensual. You're capturing people all day long who want each other, who want something, who pose in seductive ways. I can't imagine *not* thinking about sex, or them having it." His lips curved in a wry grin. "And there's nothing wrong with being a dirty pervert. Well, unless you're looking at their photos when they're gone and getting off to them, or diddling yourself while taking their pictures."

I balled up my napkin and tossed it at him. He caught it with one hand as I said, "I don't diddle myself in front of them."

He wiggled his brows. "You can diddle yourself in front of me though."

A ribbon of heat unfurled in me, and my laughter ceased. "I want that too. I want you to watch me, Adam. I want to be the one someone's looking at."

His hazel eyes darkened, that heat I'd seen last night flickering in an instant. "I know. I love your list. I love what's on it. And, Nina, you need to know—your list is what I like too."

I shuddered, both turned on and emotional all at once. This moment was so intimate, almost too intimate. "It is? I thought you were only doing it that way for me."

He inched closer. "For starters, I'd do it that way for you. But in a most happy coincidence, I like it rough too. I like it hard. I like it dirty. And I like giving a woman exactly what she wants."

His words weaved through my insides, warming me

up in ways I hadn't expected. They turned me on, but they also made me want to turn to him, to draw him close. I had to deflect, or I'd lose sight of the boundaries we'd erected.

"And you like that it's just sex," I said quickly, my pitch rising. "You aren't into relationships. Well, not after Rose."

He took a minute before answering, and I worked my way through more of my breakfast. "She wasn't my finest moment," he said carefully. "Sometimes I look back and wonder what I missed. What I should have done differently to avoid that kind of person and the lies she spun. But I was drawn to her from the start, and that was the trouble."

"What drew you to her?" I asked, hating talking about his ex, but desperately needing to understand him in a new way, to delve into this side of him that I'd never wanted to explore so fully before.

Staring off in the distance, his jaw ticked, then he turned to me. "She had this way about her where she could talk about anything, take on any topic. She was outgoing, and it was alluring," he said, and I made a note of that. I was not outgoing. I took my time with people, watching and observing before I let them in. "And that made it easy to fall under her spell. It seemed at first like we had a lot in common."

All of sudden, a plume of jealousy burned inside of me. Did he mean in the bedroom? I had to know. Even if it would hurt. "In bed, you mean?"

He met my gaze, his eyes full of nothing but the honesty I knew from him. "Yes. Does that bother you?"

I swallowed the stone in my throat, then lied. "No." For some strange reason I wanted to be the only one who liked it the way he did. The way *we* did.

But Adam surprised me again when he reached for my hand and threaded his fingers through mine. "But she never had the courage to write anything down. She never had the bravery to tell me how she wanted it. You do, and it's so insanely attractive," he said in that growly, alpha voice he'd used last night.

A voice that perhaps he only used with me.

"Everything about you is attractive. Remember that. You're honest. She was a liar, so don't compare yourself to her," he said, running a finger down my nose.

And I was busted.

He'd seen through my questions.

He knew why I'd asked.

And he could tell I wanted to be different than she was.

He'd given me what I needed to hear, and I wanted to do the same for him. I laced our fingers more tightly. "It wasn't your fault—what she did. What she took from you," I said, our eyes holding. "She was a junkie. They weave their wicked magic. They seduce. And she was beautiful, and she was sweet," I said, and though it was true, the truth tasted bitter on my tongue. But I had to endure it for him, to remind him that he wasn't to blame. "We can't erase our pasts, Adam. We can only make different choices. So you're making a different one now. To stay away from relationships, from the hurt they might inflict."

"I am," he said, and it sounded like a solemn vow. "I

trusted her, Nina. Trusted her in my home, in my life, with my heart. And she violated all of that. It's safer this way."

I nodded, getting him completely. I'd chosen safety too, for years, and in choosing him for my list, I would remain cocooned in that security.

Friendship was our safety net. We'd jump from the sky, and the net of our friendship would catch us.

"But you know what?" he added. "She is the past. Let's focus on the present. And the present, as they say, is a gift. So how about I give you a gift before I leave for work?"

11

NINA

He cleared the table in seconds flat.

He told me to strip to nothing as he left the room.

I did, anticipation rushing over my body as I removed my clothes, setting my glasses on the end table in the living room.

When he returned, one hand behind his back, I wore only my birthday suit, and his eyes shone with ravenous lust as he stared at my breasts for the first time.

He drank me in with his dirty gaze. As his eyes traveled over me, I felt consumed. Devoured.

To be wanted like this was wholly new.

And absolutely incredible.

"You are so unbelievably beautiful," he said in a smoky rasp.

"So are you," I whispered, and the admission surprised me. I'd always known he was handsome, but this time I *felt* it. I felt it in my core, in my heart. I experienced the attraction to him, and it didn't scare me. It thrilled me.

"Get on the table. On your back, dirty girl. Spread your legs open for me. Let me see if you want a gift or not. If you don't, I'll just leave."

I gasped, and pleasure ripped through my body as he taunted me. I wanted his gift. Wanted it terribly. And I didn't want him to be disappointed in what he saw. Heat pooled between my legs, making me wetter.

I perched on the edge of the table, like I was posing. I wasn't going to scoot unceremoniously or climb like a dork. I knew how to pose, how to move. And I could adjust myself too.

Like that, with my body long, I leaned my head back, letting my hair cascade down to the table, my neck stretching. I could no longer see him, but I could hear him.

His noises were animalistic. Groans of admiration.

I felt sexy as he stared at my body while I moved like water, fluidly, lowering my back, sliding along the table, stretching across it, like I'd encouraged my clients to do.

My back bowed, and I raised one knee.

A new wave of pleasure washed over me from the pose. It was a familiar boudoir shot, a woman all curved and sensual. But I was on the other side of the lens and he was the camera. He gazed at me like a man possessed.

Then he spoke, low and powerful. "Touch yourself, so I can taste if you're ready for me to stay."

My hand slid down my body, and I stroked myself, bucking the second I made contact with my sensitive flesh. It was torture and relief at the same time—all I wanted was more touch, more contact.

I held out my hand to him, and he stalked over, grabbed my wrist, and licked my finger. He moaned as he sucked off my wetness.

"Good," he growled, then he returned to where he'd stood in full view of me. "But that's not enough."

"What else should I do?"

"You know what to do, dirty girl." He parked his hands on the edge of the wood, his stare hot, branding me. "*Show. Me.*"

I quivered.

Vulnerability rippled over me as I lowered my hands between my legs, setting my palms on my thighs. But with vulnerability came something new—possibility.

By offering myself, he could give me what I craved.

I opened my legs wider, parting them with my own hands. Like I was offering him my body, my desire.

And the evidence of it.

For the briefest of seconds, he closed his eyes, like this was all too intense, seeing me like this. My worry spiked.

"Adam," I whispered, my pitch rising.

His eyes snapped open. "We're good, Nina."

I relaxed again. That was all I needed in these moments when the games, the fantasies became too much for me. When he shed that rough exterior and returned to the man I knew, the man I trusted. I had his assurance, and I was good too.

He shifted once again to the after-dark alpha who enthralled me.

Like a predator, he surveyed his prey. I was the hunted and I wanted to be ravaged. Stepping closer, he moved his hand from behind his back and dropped a hard black item and a small bottle onto the table.

I gasped. I'd known what was coming because it was my fantasy, detailed in black and white in my notebook, but I didn't know how he pulled it off. "That's not mine. How did you get that toy?"

"Amazon Prime. Two-hour delivery. Came this morning when you were in the shower. Now let's get you coming on my mouth, dirty girl." His hands circled my ankles, and he pushed my legs apart even farther. "Stay like that. I don't want you to move. Are we clear?"

I nodded. "So clear."

"Keep your hands on your thighs. Keep your legs spread nice and wide."

"Yes," I said, tingles spreading over my body as I grew wetter, hotter.

Then he bent his face to my ankle, pressed a kiss there that sent sparks across my whole body. My God, if a kiss on my ankle did that to me, what would happen when his face was between my legs?

I'd have the answer in seconds, because he traveled quickly, licking a line up my calf, over the back of my knee, along my thigh. He reached my hand, kissing me there before coming close, so damn close to where I wanted him. But not all the way. He flicked his tongue inches from my core, then moved to the other side, licking down my leg.

I was shaking from the pleasure.

He hadn't even put his mouth on me, and I was trembling with need.

"Please," I murmured.

"Beg for it."

"Adam, please. Please touch me. Please go down on me."

"Use your words," he instructed. "Use your dirty words."

I breathed in deep, and then said words I'd only said in my fantasies. "Please eat me. I'm begging you. Go down on me, and fuck me with your tongue."

In a second, his face was between my legs, and I moaned so loudly I was sure Miss Sheridan would wink at me later, tell me she'd caught my cries on her down-ward-facing-dog video.

I didn't care.

Because I was having something spectacular for the first time.

This was why women loved being eaten.

It was *decadent*.

Adam's tongued lapped me up, his mouth caressed me, his fingers stroked me. He ate me and kissed me and lavished pleasure all over my wet, aching center.

"Yes, please. Oh God. Adam," I said, writhing and arching against him, keeping my hands on my legs the whole time, as he'd told me to.

How had I missed out on this for all these years? This was better than chocolate, better than music, better than the sexiest photos I'd ever taken.

I was having what my clients were having, I was sure.

And Adam was taking me, eating me like I was the best thing he'd ever tasted.

I was close, so close, and as pleasure coiled in me, I

was terrified for the briefest of seconds that I'd come too hard, too loud.

"Adam," I cried out, my voice breaking. "I'm about to come."

He stopped. Instantly. "No."

I trembled, staring at him, the pending crush of pleasure threatening to take over. "No?"

"Beg me," he said with narrowed eyes. "Beg me to let you come."

With my hands on my thighs, I spread my legs even wider, my climax fighting to break free. I had to come. I needed the release. "Please let me come, Adam. Please. I'm begging you."

"One more 'please.'"

"Please!"

He returned to my sex and the second his lips were in their rightful place, I detonated. I screamed. I rocked and writhed and came harder than I'd ever come before as white-hot pleasure ripped through me. I was seeing stars upon galaxies of stars.

And it wasn't stopping.

Nor was he. He slowed his pace, but kept licking, kept kissing. Somewhere in the back of my mind, I registered a sound. A bottle being opened. A squirt.

He pulled his mouth away. "Keep your hands on your thighs. I'm not done with you."

Shuddering, I whispered, "Yes."

Then I felt his fingers traveling lower, farther. When he reached my ass, he pushed, and I tensed. "I've got you."

And oh yes, did he ever have me.

He pushed the tip of his lubricated finger into my ass, and I squirmed, letting out a yelp. "Adam, Adam, Adam," I panted, my voice rising because as much as I wanted this, as much as I trusted him, his finger was entering my rear, and this was also very much virgin territory.

"Do you need me to stop?" he asked, stilling himself.

I drew a breath, shook my head. "No." Then, louder this time, I told him exactly what I wanted. Because this was on my list too. "I want you to keep going."

"That's my girl," he said, praising me as he pushed his finger deeper. He pressed a kiss to my sensitive clit, and my hips rocked up in pleasure.

"So nice and tight," he murmured against me as he stroked inside me with his finger. "Have you taken anything in your ass before, sweet girl?"

Sweet girl.

He'd used that nickname for the second time, and somehow it felt fitting as he touched me there. I loved that he still saw me as sweet even as he explored all my entrances.

"Yes. Just a plug though," I admitted.

"Good. This will feel so much better," he said, slowly easing out his finger.

I craned my neck as he reached for the black vibrator, hit the on button, and pressed it against my ass.

I jerked, a wave of lust spilling over me as he slid the tip of the toy against my ass.

"God, yes. That's so good."

"It's going to be so damn good when you beg to come again."

That was all he said, because he silenced himself with me. His lips returned to my swollen center, his tongue flicking my clit as he pushed the toy deeper into my rear.

The twin sensations—penetration and filthy kisses—sent me into the stratosphere in seconds.

Lust rocketed through me, and I became a wild woman. Swallowed whole by pleasure, I gave in to the crush of sensations. To the waves of desire flooding my body. I felt tight and hot on the vibrator and wet and soft on his mouth.

And I felt bliss.

Tingling, delicious bliss racing across my skin.

I was close again, and I remembered the rules.

"Adam, let me come."

He growled against me. He didn't even have to say a word. I knew what he wanted me to do—what *I wanted to do.*

"Please," I keened as I reached the edge, and he sent me over, driving me into ecstatic oblivion with toy and tongue.

I was in another world, another land, and I floated there on a sea of euphoria for minutes.

I was nothing but breaths and pants and contented moans.

And as I came back into my body, I was vaguely aware that it was my turn, that I wanted to do something for him.

But he rose, placing a finger to my lips as he shook his head. "I know what you want. You can suck me off when I come home from work."

"Yes," I said, because that was my answer to everything with him. A loud, reverberating *yes*.

Then he took me to the shower, stripping off his jeans, turning on the water, and scanning the shelf quickly. "Do you have a shower cap? So you don't get your gorgeous hair wet?"

I laughed softly. "No, I don't have one. I use hair ties. On the vanity."

He stepped out of the stall, giving me a bird's-eye view of his sculpted ass. My friend had a fantastic body. One I wanted to lick and kiss and bite. He reached for a tie on the vanity then returned to the shower, shutting the glass door.

He proffered a black band for my hair, and I smiled as I looped up my brown locks in a messy bun. He murmured appreciatively.

Then he washed me.

He was attentive, soaping my shoulders, my back, my belly, and making sure my messy bun didn't get wet. That was no easy task, but he pulled it off. A little thing, but I was grateful, because no woman wants to do her hair twice in an hour.

He let me take my turn, soaping his strong arms, his chest, his carved abs.

We were quiet in the shower, wordlessly caring for each other. Showing a new type of touch—one I hadn't foreseen when I penned my list. *Care.*

Questions swirled in my head. Where did we go from here? Did this mean something different? This surprisingly tender moment in the shower? When touch was no longer sexual, but still intimate in an entirely new way?

I had no answers, and I didn't want to ask him, but I could feel those questions echoing in my head, a space that was already filled with so many unknowns.

After, when he was dressed and ready for work, my uncertainty descended again briefly. Should I kiss him goodbye? Walk him to the door? I wasn't sure what we were supposed to do next or how we should behave. But I remembered our breakfast and how easy it was, and I returned to that. *To us.*

"Thanks for breakfast. Best I've ever had."

"Funny, I was going to say the same about my dish," he said with a wink.

My heart warmed. We could do this. We could be *us.*

But the moment was broken when his phone rang.

12

ADAM

Brandon's face appeared on my phone as The Rolling Stones' *"Start Me Up"* blasted.

He'd picked that tune. It was his favorite, and it was our anthem during college. The Friday night song, we'd called it, before we hit the quad for parties, pool, and whatever else we could find when it came to festivities.

I slid my thumb across the screen, answering, "You can't resist me. Admit it. This is the second time in less than twenty-four hours you've called."

"Yes, that's it, Adam. I can't stay away from you," he said, and his eyes drifted to Nina at the edge of the screen. *"Bonjour, Mademoiselle Nina. Ça va?"*

She laughed, rolling her eyes. She didn't know Brandon well, but she'd met him a year ago when he was in town. "Do you actually speak French now?"

I shot her a knowing look. "Remember last time Brandon was here? He tried to pick up some gals from Montreal using his French skills, and he failed abysmally."

"Is that so?" she asked. I liked that she was chatting with him on this call, even briefly, because she was normally reserved with people she didn't know well. Brandon fell into that category. But here she was, by my side. That was a sign that she wasn't weirded out by what we'd just done. She was still herself with me, and that reassured me that we could work through her list exactly as we intended to.

Brandon cleared his throat. "Ahem. It wasn't my French that failed me. Don't you remember?"

I smacked my palm to my forehead, recalling how his pickup attempt went down—in flames. "That's right. It was your radar that failed you. The Montreal gals weren't in Vegas for the boys. They were in Vegas for the girls."

"All the more reason why I was trying to insert myself into their lady sandwich," he said, flashing a grin, keeping it light, as he always did. I knew better, but I also knew this was how he operated. How he had to operate.

"Dream big, my friend," I said, then shifted gears. "To what do I owe the pleasure of an early morning phone call?"

Brandon furrowed his brow, casting his gaze from Nina to me and back. "Isn't it eight-thirty where you are? I know you two are like Batman-and-Robin kind of close, but I didn't realize you were hanging out in the bat cave that early."

"For the record, I'm not Robin, and besides, this is *my* bat cave," Nina said, arching a brow over her glasses. I reined in a grin, both from the comment—because who in their right mind ever wanted to be Robin?—and also because she looked badass in her red-as-sin glasses and with that sharp stare in her brown eyes. And tough, too, with her whole photographer look in full force this morning. Dark jeans, black boots, and a wine-red shirt. Biker chic, and did she ever wear it well.

She wore everything well, including her kinks. To think the woman who'd been my friend and neighbor had been hiding this fantastic secret these last few years, and I didn't mean her virginity. I meant her appetite in bed—she was a little bit submissive, a lot kinky, and all kinds of dirty.

My kind of woman.

And I was the only one who knew about the other side of Nina.

"Fine, you can be Catwoman and he can be Batman. How's that?" Brandon asked, and his tone was still inquisitive, but I doubted he wanted to know what we thought of his superhero assignments. The way he glanced from Nina to me and back again suggested he was still trying to get a read on us. "Anyway, what are you two comic book characters up to?" he asked.

Nina smiled for a sliver of a second, like it escaped her lips and she had to catch it before it sprinted away from her. Then she schooled her expression, but I could read between the lines. She was keeping our little tryst a secret, and relishing, too, that we were having one.

Same here.

I reveled in our secret.

"I'm on my way to work, and Nina is too," I said to Brandon, giving the simplest reply. "And to answer your

other question, you nosy bastard, I've been staying with
Nina for the last few nights, since my place is being
painted. What's up with you? I need to head to the car,
so I don't have long."

"Funny, I don't either. I have a few meetings, then I
have to pack because I happen to have a plane to catch .
. ." He let his voice trail off, like he had something up his
sleeve.

"Where are you headed?"

He took a beat. "To Vegas, as a matter of fact. And if
you play your cards right, I just might let the two of you
take me out for a night on the town. How's that for
generous?"

I grinned. "That's great that you'll be here."

Nina leaned in close. "We'd love that. We'd be happy
to see you. You have to join us."

"We?" Brandon's eyebrows shot into his hairline.
"Are you two a *we* and I'm just learning now?"

The smile on her face disappeared instantly. She
blushed, turning the shade of a fire engine. She pressed
a hand to her cheek and stepped away from the frame,
whispering, "*Sorry.*"

No way. No way was I going to let her feel like she
had to apologize.

I told Brandon I'd be right back, then I muted the
call and set down the phone on the entryway table.

I closed the distance, cupped her cheek. "Nina, you
have nothing to be sorry for."

She shook her head, like she was mad at herself. "I
shouldn't have said that. I shouldn't have acted like *we*

were a thing, or like we did things together." It came out in a whisper.

I tilted my head. "But we do. We do hang out together. And we will keep doing that. You know that, don't you?"

But her shoulders still radiated tension. Her jaw was set hard. I tucked a finger under her chin, raising her face. "We're good. I promise."

She let out a long gust of breath. "Please know I wasn't trying to suggest anything. It just came out. I guess because you've been staying here this week, and we got into a rhythm with the dinners and everything." She laughed, but it sounded forced. "Anyway, I know we're not a *we*. We're just friends, and it will be so fun to see Brandon as friends."

She flashed me a smile that didn't quite reach her eyes, then she shoved my shoulder like a pal would do. "Go finish with Brandon. He needs you."

I swiped my thumb over her chin. "He's doing well. I swear. Last time I saw him, he was definitely himself again."

"Good," she said with a smile. "I've been hoping he would be."

"But are you okay?" I pressed.

"I'm good. We're good. I swear. I need to get ready for my client."

But were we good? Was she? I couldn't read her. Couldn't tell if she was covering something up.

For the first time since we'd been friends, I wasn't sure how to proceed. So I reverted to the other thing we were—temporary lovers. Leaning on that, I curled a hand around her head and whispered roughly, "I'll see you tonight, and when I do, you're going to get on your knees, just the way you want."

A tremble seemed to vibrate across her body. Her chocolate eyes sparkled. There. I'd restored our balance by focusing on the mission—her list. The decadent, fantastic list that I was lucky enough to work on.

God bless women and their to-do-loving minds.

Grabbing the phone, I headed for the door and unmuted it, returning to Brandon.

Brandon stared, wide-eyed, like he was tapping his toe. "Oh, hi. How are you? Good to see you again. I did all my banking and taxes and emails while you were gone. So, ahem, what was *that?*"

"What was what?" I asked, as if I didn't know.

His eyebrow rose. "That was, like, a minute-long conversation. *On mute.*" He tapped his chin, like he was deep in thought. "Gee, I wonder. Are you involved with her?"

Pushing open the stairwell, I headed for the steps so I could have this talk in private, though I didn't intend to tell him a single thing Nina had confided in me. Well, she'd only confided in me *after* I'd stumbled across the treasure map to her desire. But even so, she'd shared something private, and I wasn't about to serve it up to anyone. If Nina chose to tell her friends, that was one thing. It wasn't my info to share.

"No, but I had something I needed to talk to her about that didn't pertain to you. What brings you to Vegas? How long will you be in town?"

"*Didn't 'pertain' to me?* Aren't you fancy?"

I rolled my eyes. "Answers, man, answers."

"I arrive Saturday morning. Last-minute meetings at the big convention in town. Didn't expect to be going, but alas, plans change. I'll be there for a couple of days, then I'm heading to Los Angeles for a shoot. A commercial I'm doing for a watchmaker." Brandon was a top-notch cinematographer, working for advertisers all over the world.

"Need a place to stay here? Mine is being painted, but they should be done by then."

"I don't want to cramp your style. I'm sure I can find some dingy cut-rate motel off the Strip."

I rolled my eyes. "The offer stands."

"*Merci.*" His expression shifted to serious. "Listen, if you're not involved with Nina, what do you think about me—"

"No." One word. Sharp as a knife.

He cracked up, pointing at me, laughing his head off. "You are so busted. The way you flew off the handle was brilliant. Does she know you're secretly in love with her?"

I bounded down the steps, scoffing at his assessment. He was wrong. Dead wrong. That feeling in my chest last night wasn't love. It was . . . what was it? I snapped my fingers, finding the answer. *Affection.* Yeah, that sounded about right. Naturally I'd feel affection for a good friend. Not love. Besides, my heart was in time-out after Rose, and the clock hadn't wound down yet. "First of all, I'm not in love with her. I'm not in *anything* with her. But I still don't want you hitting on her," I said.

"And why's that?"

I wasn't going to tell him the nitty-gritty, but I could still be honest. "Because you're a layover. And she's not that kind of girl. She's not into hookups," I said, confident that what Nina and I were doing was not a hookup.

We were having a moment to work through her wishes.

A bucket list was born out of need, not out of an itch to scratch.

He lifted an eyebrow. "Then, once you do find the balls to make your move, you'd better make sure you're not a hookup."

"Again, I'm not making any moves. She's a friend. Just a friend."

He moved closer to the screen. "Sure, for now. But even through the haze of FaceTime, I can tell by the way you look at her. Don't forget—I record emotions for a living, and yours are written all over your face. You might want to deal with that sooner rather than later."

"Thanks for the unsolicited advice," I said robotically. "Please remember to check it at the door next time."

He smiled, a gregarious grin I knew well. "C'mon. It's what I do, man. I tell you the truth because that's my job. That's what we do for each other. You've always called me out on my bullshit when it comes to women and work and life. Hell, how many times have you told me I need to move on?"

I sighed heavily, letting go of my annoyance. How could I harbor any frustration when the man mentioned, even without saying her name, the woman he'd lost? The reason he'd hit on the gals from Montreal last year was he knew he wasn't going home with them. He hadn't gone home with anyone since his long-time girlfriend had died three years ago in a fatal car wreck. He'd simply covered up his pain with harmless flirting that went nowhere. But lately, he'd seemed better, happier, more together.

I leveled him with a stare. "I say it because I want you to be happy again, you miserable bastard. I want you to find a sliver of what you once had."

"That'll never happen."

"Do you really believe that?" I asked, hoping he'd say no.

He just shrugged, and I hated that a part of him did believe it. I'd do nearly anything to help him find that place again where he could be happy.

"Look, Brand. I get it. What happened was devastating, no denying that," I said, because the man splintered in a million pieces when he lost Jenna. But he'd steadily been picking himself up, finding ways to enjoy life. Taking off to live in Paris was part of that, escaping from the memories of his life here in Vegas with his longtime girl. I missed him, but I'd hoped the new location was exactly what he'd needed to move through his grief. Only, I didn't know if he'd truly made a life there. "And when you're ready, you'll be ready," I added. "But I hope for your sake it's soon, because it would be awesome to see you with a legit smile again."

He flashed another half grin. "I'm happy enough. And I'll be happy for you when you face your feelings for your Robin. Or your Catwoman. Whatever she is to you. See you this weekend," he said with a smile and ended the call.

As I stared at the blank screen, I shook my head, talking back to the emptiness. "There's nothing to face," I said, and I believed it. I had to believe it. Feelings weren't part of the equation. They couldn't be. Nina didn't want them. I was allergic to them. Besides, I didn't want to play Batman and Robin with her.

When I hopped into my Tesla, my phone dinged with a text message. I slid it open to find the painter updating me.

David the Painter: *We will be there shortly! We should be finished by tomorrow at the latest.*

I sent a quick thanks and pulled out of the garage, running through options this weekend for our regular crew of friends, plus Brandon. The club we all liked at The Luxe, a nearby pool hall, or maybe dinner at a swank eatery in The Cosmopolitan.

Would Nina and I go out as clandestine lovers or friends once more? Would we be done with her list by then?

My muscles tightened at the thought, but I shook it off as I headed into the office.

Her list was full of items, and we'd tackle them all.

Including number eleven.

I'd find a way to make all her wishes come true.

That was what I wanted for Nina. *For my friend.* The woman deserved the world. She deserved to know, too, that I was still the man she could trust, that I hadn't run off and told Brandon anything at all.

After I said hello to my employees, I shut my office door and picked up my phone.

13

ADAM

I tapped out a simple text.

Adam: Hey you.

Nina: Hi.

Adam: I need you to know—I won't say a word to anyone. What we did is personal. I'm not the type of guy who brags and you are NOT a conquest.

Nina: Thank you. Also, I know you're not that type of guy.

Adam: But I do know you're close to your friends, so if you want to share with them, I have no issues with that. I get that women like to share.

Nina: Got it. I have the seal of approval to tell Lily and Kate you have a big d-i-c-k.

Nina: Oops!

Nina: Wherever did that naughty side of me come from?

Adam: That naughty side *is* you, Nina. By the way, this morning was absolutely amazing.

Nina: It was for me. But was it for you?

Adam: Couldn't you tell how much I loved it?

Nina: I think, but in all honesty, I'm still figuring this out. Everything is new to me.

I leaned back in my chair, rereading that, letting the enormity of her words sink in. Her question was normal, something any woman would ask of her man, and a man of his woman. But with Nina, there was a whole other layer. She didn't have any history to compare me to. And I loved that. I craved being her first everything. And this was a first for her too—talking about what she'd done. Not only had she let me in, now she was letting me in her head in another way. And I wanted to honor that and give her what she needed too.

Adam: Let me help you figure this out. You shouldn't just "think" I loved it. I want you to be certain. Without a shadow of a doubt. Close your eyes and remember how I stared at every inch of your exquisite body like a man possessed. How I devoured your perfect pink pussy like I was starving. Nina, I wanted my face covered in your juices. I still do. I could lick you all day. The only thing to figure out is how quickly I can get my mouth on your sweetness again, because I am rock hard right now.

Nina: Well, that *does* seem to answer my question. Thank you for knowing what I needed. And thanks for making me need to go change my panties again because they're soaked now.

Adam: As they should be when you talk to me. And now that we're clear on how I loved every single second of going down on you, I want you to tell me where your head is about last night, about this morning. I want to know how you're doing.

She didn't respond right away. But the three flashing dots indicated she was typing, and considering how long they flickered, she must have been typing a lot. But when her reply arrived, it was short. To the point.

Nina: This is where my head is—what do you think of me now?

I sat up straight. Dragged a hand through my hair. Was she worried I'd think differently of her? That wouldn't do.

Adam: I think you're beautiful and sexy, and I love that you know your own mind. That you want to explore your body. I love that you're taking charge of your pleasure. And I feel like the luckiest man in the whole damn city to be the one to help you. Does that make it clear where my head is?

Nina: I think so. Also, I can't stop thinking about the table.

Adam: I can't either. You were spectacular. You come so gloriously. It's incredible watching you.

Nina: I like to watch you too when you touch me.

Adam: Yeah? You liked looking at my face between your legs?

Nina: I loved it. Loved the way you looked when you devoured me.

Of course she loved to watch. She was the observer. And she was dead-on with her summation.

Adam: Did you take pictures with your mind's eye?

Nina: They're in my head. They don't stop playing.

Adam: Don't I know that? You are all I can picture right now. I should be working through my call list, but instead I'm seeing your lush body spread across the table. I can still hear your noises, I can feel your smooth skin, and I can still taste you. You taste like heaven, Nina.

Nina: I want to know what you taste like. All of you. I want to feel you in my mouth. I want to take you deep in my throat and watch the expressions on your face as you come.

I dropped my forehead to my hand. I was an inferno. How was I going to make it through this day? The images in my mind were obscene, just the way I liked them, and just the way that would distract me all day long.

Adam: Woman, I am so goddamn hard right now, and I have to go to a meeting in fifteen minutes. And I don't want to stop with you. All I want to do is tell you how much more I want to do to you and with you.

Nina: I want you to do everything.

I swallowed roughly as I read that last one again and again. I wanted to do everything with her. Every last thing. And since we were being so open about our bedroom wishes, I needed to open the door for her to back out. That was the last thing I wanted in the universe, but I cared too much about her not to ask. I had to.

Adam: Are you still good with this? Do you still feel okay about working through your list? What you told me this morning stayed with me. It resonated. I listened. We don't have to cross that line if you don't want to.

Nina: Adam, I'm so good with this. I promise you. I'm ready. I feel like I'm finally breaking free of my head.

Adam: Your head must be a wondrous and filthy place.

Nina: It is. That's the good and bad of it. I've lived all my sexuality in my mind and in my bed by myself. I've only ever had sex with myself and with my fantasies.

And now my fantasies are becoming reality. It's like I'm understanding who I am in a whole new way.

This was another text that called for a second read, a third, a fourth. Because this one touched a different part of me. It touched my mind. It touched my heart that cared deeply for this woman. And it stirred up something new for me too—a deep and powerful sense of privilege. It was such a privilege to be the one she trusted. I never wanted to betray that trust.

Adam: Who you are is incredible, and I want to be the one to help you explore all your desires. So I'm going to ask now, and I'll ask again tonight, because I want you to be 100 percent certain—here goes. Will you give me your virginity tonight?

14

NINA

He didn't say *fuck*.

Or *sleep with me* or *make love to me*. There would be no making love. I didn't want that. We weren't those kinds of people.

But even though I liked it hard and rough, I also discovered something new as I read his last message.

Every now and then, I liked a little tenderness. Maybe it was the occasional soft kiss like he gave me before bed, or perhaps it was his devoted touch, like in the shower this morning. Or maybe it came in the form of words.

Like now.

Will you give me your virginity?

He didn't say he wanted to take it.

He wanted me to give it. And give it to him. He knew it was my body, my innocence to give away. It wasn't his to take. It wasn't anyone's to take. It belonged to me, and I had the power to choose when to walk away from it.

He understood that deeply.

That was what his question told me. In a message about sex, I saw there was so much more to this man. And I feared when I gave my virginity to him, the act might be more than sex for me.

I'd have to do everything I could to focus on the physical, and only the physical.

Thank God I had a shoot in a few minutes. That was what I needed. Bodies, images, pictures. A world I knew intimately.

Me in my zone. The more time I spent in a space I knew well, the better off I'd be later tonight. Because I didn't want to lose myself when I entered new territory with Adam.

Photography would center me, as it always had.

I didn't need to write a long reply.

All he needed was one word. And one word was all I gave. It said everything.

Nina: Yes.

* * *

Today the woman wore white. Stockings, garters, white lace panties, and a demi-cup bra.

"You look like an angel," I told Melanie, who'd arranged the shoot as a surprise gift for her bride-to-be.

"I feel so awkward," my client confessed as she sat rigidly on the lush cranberry-colored velvet lounge in my studio.

"I know that feeling well," I said with a soft smile. "But this is a safe place. You look beautiful, and I want you to feel beautiful for your shoot. So, we can do that a couple of ways. One is wine."

She laughed. "I like wine, but it *is* only ten in the morning."

"True, wine o'clock doesn't usually start till after noon. So here's the other." I stepped away from the couch, headed for the nightstand in my studio, and reached into a drawer. I took out a photo album. I kept it here for this very reason—when clients had a crisis of confidence.

"What do you have there?" Her curiosity was piqued.

"I'll show you," I said, returning to the lounge, where I flipped it open for her.

She brought her hand to her mouth and laughed at the first page.

"Exactly. Let it all out," I said, encouraging her.

"I'm sorry, but that's so funny."

"That's why I included it."

I looked down at the page and the pictures of myself in a red bra and panty set. They were self-portraits, shots of me trying to look sexy and failing miserably. All the shots that would never see the light of day were in here. The ones where I squinted or made duck lips, or where my sexy pose looked more like a crab walk.

"This is the clay. The rough, unmade clay."

She nodded as I moved through the pages, shot after unusable shot. "I see where you're going."

"We need the clay to make the sculpture." I flipped to the final one.

The *pièce de résistance*.

Me, stretched out on this very couch, my head leaning back, my hair tumbling over the pillow. My back arched. Breasts perking up. Skin shimmering. A look of bliss in my eyes.

Just like how I felt this morning on the table with Adam.

A faint shudder ran through me as I remembered posing like this for him. With that memory front and center, I saw my self-portrait in a new light. I understood intrinsically the expression on my own face. I knew what it was like to want and to want so powerfully it was written in your eyes.

I *wanted* like that woman in the photo.

And I'd *had*.

Tonight, I would have even more. I'd have it all.

Melanie's laughter faded, replaced by a sort of wonder as she gazed at the shot. "That's what I want Josie to feel when she looks at the pictures. This is how she makes me feel," she said reverently, running a hand over the image.

"She's going to be enthralled. And so are you. And if I have to take five hundred shots to get the perfect one, I will."

She shot me the most grateful grin. "Thank you." Her eyes returned to my photo. "When you took this photo of yourself, what was going through your mind? What were you thinking of?"

I had no idea. But I had every idea too.

"I was imagining what it felt like to want someone desperately. To want to experience every bit of bliss with that person," I said, speaking the full truth now, and it felt fantastic. Another taste of freedom.

"I know exactly what you mean," she said.

She was ready.

She didn't transform into a runway model, but she settled into her body, enjoying the attention, imagining the camera was Josie, I suspected, as she let all her desires play in her eyes.

She was gorgeous, and I was the lucky photographer who captured it.

Even more so, for the first time, I understood how she felt.

When Melanie was finished and dressed in her slacks and a pretty white blouse, I walked her to the door and out into the hall. "I'll send you edits soon. You're going to love it, and she's going to be over the moon."

"Thank you. I can't imagine anyone else taking those shots of me. You made that all possible."

"You did," I corrected her.

After Melanie stepped into the waiting elevator that whisked her downstairs, I walked toward my condo. Before I reached the door, a smoky, sexy voice called out.

"You are a tech wizard."

I laughed at the sound of Miss Sheridan and swiveled around. "I better get a wizard hat, then."

She beamed, patting her platinum-blonde hair and shaking her hips. The showgirl in her ran strong. "My last video was so popular I had thousands of new views this morning alone."

"No one does yoga better than you."

She walked in my direction, with the confidence of her stage days enrobing her. "But that's not why I popped out to see you," she said, her eyes dancing with mischief.

Uh-oh.

"I saw Adam pick up a package this morning."

My jaw threatened to drop. Please, dear God, let the vibrator not have arrived in *Joy Delivered* packaging.

"I don't know what was in the package," she added, and I contained the naughty grin that threatened to appear. *I knew* what was in the package, and it had already been in me.

"But the look on his face . . ." she said, trailing off.

Oh my. I bet he was indeed pleased with his ordering skills.

"He seemed quite happy," she continued, wiggling her brows as she reached me.

Keeping our battery-assisted secrets to myself, I answered with a polite "He's a happy guy."

She patted my shoulder. "You kids today. Do I just need to call a spade a spade? He seemed happy in the way that a man does after . . ."

Had she heard us? The walls were insulated. Was I that loud?

She seemed to sense my worries.

"Sweetheart, I don't know what happens behind your closed door. I don't know what was in that package. I didn't hear anything, but I don't have to. I can tell there's something between the two of you, and I think it's fantastic. I love seeing young people get together. It's why I love this city. So many people coming together."

Butterflies fluttered in my chest, and for a split second, I imagined an *us*. Adam and me. Possibilities beyond my list dared to flash before my eyes. Breakfasts and dinners and nights out.

Where were these errant thoughts coming from?

They were as invasive as the thoughts of sex had been yesterday morning.

And they were a real risk too.

That was precisely what I needed to avoid—catching feelings. Getting ahead of the list.

"Nothing is happening," I assured her, and then I vowed to assure myself of that all day long.

Because the butterflies I felt at her mere suggestion were never going to be set free.

15

NINA

That afternoon, I met my girlfriends at our favorite coffee shop and ordered my usual.

Kate had finished work early for the day, and Lily was taking a break from a story she'd been chasing on a new rookie quarterback. She was an award-winning and nationally recognized reporter for a sports network. As for Kate, her job remained cloaked in mystery. Well, to others. I understood it perfectly, but we treated it as if she worked at the CIA.

Don't ask, don't tell.

"So all is well at corporate headquarters with your super-secret new missions?" I asked my friend with the chestnut hair and hazel eyes.

Kate shrugged playfully. "I'd tell you, but then I'd have to kill you."

Lily laughed, rolling her eyes. "You're such a clandestine operative."

"That's me," Kate added, then brought her finger to

her lips. "All of Vegas's deepest nighttime secrets are safe with me."

"Unless we can ply them out of you with drinks this weekend," I added playfully.

"Speaking of this weekend, I heard Brandon is coming to town and we're all going out," Lily remarked, flicking a strand of blonde hair off her shoulder. "Finn had lunch with Jake and Adam, and the plans came up."

"And we also have Adam's new deals to celebrate," Kate added.

Lily snapped her gaze to Kate. "How did you know?"

I wanted to ask the same question, so I was glad Lily had pounced first.

"I heard it from Jake," Kate said, looking away, my normally confident friend betraying the slightest bit of guilt. Did she have a secret thing going with Jake?

"You two have become awfully chatty." Lily jumped on that nugget, a satisfied grin on her face as she brought her latte to her lips.

Kate stared at her pointedly. "You need to stop reading something into every little thing."

Lily laughed. "But that's what a good reporter does. Picks up on clues, and you've been dropping them for a long time. You and Jake just have this vibe between you."

I cleared my throat. "It's hardly a vibe. It's more like a heatwave of sexual tension, so thick you could bottle it." I whipped out my phone and showed them a shot I'd taken of Kate and Jake dancing at Lily's recent wedding. The best man and the maid of honor. Even though he held her at arm's length, and even though the shot wasn't a close-up, it was impossible to miss the smolder in his eyes as he stared at the brunette beauty.

Kate waved a hand dismissively, taking a drink of her coffee. "I assure you there is nothing brewing between us. But speaking of brewing," she said, turning to me, "how is it living with sexy, charming, better-than-the-boy-next-door Adam?"

Those damn butterflies had the audacity to sweep through me once more.

At the mere mention of Adam's name.

Lily leaned forward and batted her lids, getting in on the fun. "Yes, do tell. I'm sure it's sooo easy to spend your nights and mornings with that handsome man who treats you like a queen."

My face heated. Why was I so transparent?

Maybe because Lily and Kate were right. Adam was all those things.

And so much more, as I'd learned last night.

Last night.

It had been less than twenty-four hours since he'd found my list, and already I'd experienced an inordinate amount of morning-after tingles and far too many chest flutters. This had to stop. I had to keep everything on the sex-and-only-sex level.

And the sex so far had been better than my wildest fantasies, and my fantasies were lawless.

"He's great, and it's fun," I said in a cheery voice, squaring my shoulders.

Lily hummed, a doubtful sound. "And your eyes say otherwise."

"What do they say?"

Kate shrugged, a grin on her face. "You tell us."

And the thing was, I wanted to tell them. They were my best friends. They knew me. They understood my choices. They respected my decisions. They never pressured me to go after a guy or to try to shed my virginity with just anyone simply for the sake of losing it once and for all. All the guys I'd dated were not the right ones, and they never pushed me over cosmos or a girls' night out to ditch my V card.

Now I was twenty-four. The risks my sister had faced and surmounted weren't risks for me. I had a degree, a business, and a home I owned. That didn't mean I wanted a baby, but the teenage-pregnancy specter was long gone. And I was religious with protection. Radically religious.

But that wasn't what tonight would be about.

It wasn't about the choices I'd made back when I was in high school. It was about the freedom to make a new round of choices as a grown woman.

I was in full control of my life.

And I wanted to be in full control of my sexuality.

To own it completely.

I was ready.

And I was ready for something else.

To tell my friends, as Adam had sensed I'd want to do. He was right. I wanted to share this huge step with my girls.

I downed some of my Earl Grey latte, then took a deep breath. "Have you heard of *Ask Aphrodite*?"

They shook their heads.

I took out my phone and clicked on the episode I'd

listened to this morning, giving one AirPod to Lily and one to Kate.

A listener asked a seemingly simple question, but the more I mulled it over, the more I realized it wasn't simple at all.

The question begins like this: "How do I know when I'm ready? Truly ready to try something new? I think about kinky things all the time. I wonder what it'll feel like to explore naughtier shores. To try all sorts of risqué and daring acts. But what if I don't like it when I do?"

This is an excellent question.

Life is full of what-ifs. You don't know if you're going to like a massage before you go, and maybe you like a certain masseuse but not another. Perhaps you try a new restaurant that has rave reviews, and it falls short. Or the opposite occurs.

Sex is the same. You might love giving fellatio to one man and not to another.

Or maybe a certain lover can bring you to orgasm in ways no one else has. In places on your body you never imagined you'd want to be touched.

How do you know?

You don't know. Until you try.

And when you try, don't think of sex as failing or succeeding. Think of it as the journey to discovery.

To discovering everything you like.

As wiser people than me have said—it's not about the destination, but the journey. And enjoying the ride to your heart's and body's content.

. . .

They removed the AirPods.

Kate raised a brow, and Lily gave me a *what does this mean* look.

I drew another breath and took another step on my personal journey. "I'm sleeping with Adam tonight. We made a deal. I'm giving him my virginity because I trust him. Because I'm ready. Because it's time. And when we're done, we'll walk away as friends."

Lily choked on her latte.

Kate nearly dropped her coffee. "What? Why?"

Lily set down her drink, collecting herself before she added, "Be careful, Nina."

"I'm on protection," I said, reminding her. "You know that."

"No. I mean be careful with *this*." Lily tapped her heart.

But how could I be anything but careful? I knew the score.

All I had to do was keep my head on straight about the final destination—friendship.

That way, the journey would be filled only with pleasure.

Starting in a few more hours.

16

NINA

His text arrived shortly before seven as I emailed some shots to Marco and Evangeline. My phone vibrated next to me on my desk. I grabbed it, eager.

Adam: I'll be home in thirty minutes. On the dot. Be on your knees in the living room, waiting for me. Wear what you had on when you were on your hands and knees in bed the other night riding your toy while I slept quietly a room away.

With the phone in hand, I practically sprinted to my bedroom, yanking open the drawer with my sleep clothes. Sleep shorts and tanks, like I wore the other night. But I'd taken off the shorts and the panties. I grabbed a white tank, tossed it on the bed, then took a quick shower. When I was done, I spread cherry lotion on my legs, dusted some blush on my cheeks, and slicked on some lip gloss.

I set my glasses in their case and popped in a pair of contacts.

I checked the time.

Fifteen more minutes. I grabbed my tablet, clicking to some of my favorite photographers' pages, checking out their new work. I was always on the hunt for inspiration, whether it was new angles or styles and colors. I bookmarked a few images I liked, stopping briefly at a shot of a couple on a bed. A man kissed the hollow of a woman's throat, while she seemed to gaze knowingly at the camera. I imagined what came next, pictured them stripping each other, and saw the camera capturing it all.

But when I looked at the image again, I didn't see some unknown couple. I saw Adam and me, and I gasped then moaned.

Yes.

I wanted that.

All of that.

And I wanted him to know how much.

I checked the clock. Ten more minutes. Just enough time to give him a surprise gift.

I turned off my tablet and pulled on the white tank. It was a cropped top—it landed at my midriff. I wore nothing else. Quickly, I walked to my studio, grabbed a tripod, and returned to my living room.

I set up my phone and its camera timer, kneeled, and took a self-portrait in just the position he'd requested.

One shot. One chance. I rose and peered at the image.

Yes.

He should be pulling into the garage right now.

In one of my most daring acts ever, I sent the photo, and a wave of satisfaction rolled through me from what I'd just done.

I couldn't wait for him to walk through the door.

17

ADAM

Control was my thing.

In business school, I'd studied its value. He who keeps his composure negotiates best, and he who negotiates best gets what he wants.

At the gym every day, I practiced that control too, working out, following a regimen. Never breaking.

Tonight I'd stuck to my workout plan, weights and the treadmill. I didn't need to go soft, not when I'd be spending plenty of time in my birthday suit with the prettiest woman I'd ever known.

When I finished my routine, I sent her a text letting her know I'd be home in thirty minutes.

After a quick shower, I pulled on jeans and a T-shirt and headed to our building. As the elevator rose, my phone dinged with a reply. I slid my thumb over the screen. A multimedia image was loading, and the caption read: *I'm a good dirty girl, waiting for you like you asked.*

My mouth went dry. My chest heated.

I clicked open the photo.

My dick jumped to attention, saluting anyone and everything in the free universe.

And that was when the truth smacked me in the face.

She had all the control.

It wasn't her body, though those curves and lush skin required worship all night long. And it wasn't her face, though she was stunning in every way.

It was her daring.

It was her sexuality.

It was how she owned her wants.

She wanted me to see her before I walked in. And hell, did I ever see her. This was the most alluring photo I'd ever gazed at in my life—Nina on her knees, wearing only a tank that barely covered the bottoms of her perfect breasts. Her lips parted slightly. Her skin dewy. Her face beautiful and full of sensual desire.

This picture was the proof—she had the control. She held the power. Even if I'd be the one to tell her what to do and when to do it, she was calling all the shots.

She was the director of the theater of her desire, and I was merely her actor, playing his part.

But at least I had the starring role.

I reached her door, took out my key, and opened it.

I didn't say *Honey, I'm home* in my playful fifties husband tone.

Tonight was not for joking.

I said nothing as the door squeaked open and I entered her pleasure den. The lights were dimmed. Music pulsed, a low seductive beat that set the mood.

My eyes snapped to her immediately.

She appeared exactly as I'd asked her.

Exactly as she'd shown me in the image.

She gripped her wrists behind her back, but her body was soft, not rigid. She looked up at me with wide, expectant eyes, waiting for me to speak first.

My body sizzled as I stared at the filthy angel waiting for me to defile her. "Do you know what dirty girls get when they send naughty pictures?"

She shook her head, her voice breathless. "No. What do they get?"

I moved to her, dropped to the floor, curled a hand around the back of her head, and took her lips.

I kissed her fiercely, with all the hunger that had built all day. Hell, *all year*. I swept my mouth over hers and consumed her lips, kissing her exactly how we both liked. She moaned into my mouth as I lowered my hand between her legs, sliding my fingers across her hot, wetness.

My God, she was a divine creature. So aroused already. So wet so soon.

Control yourself.

As much as I wanted to play with her with my fingers, that wasn't what I planned to do first. I needed to give her something else.

I rose, jerked off my T-shirt, and unzipped my jeans.

Her eyes lit up like sparklers. She licked her lips, such an eager girl, ready to please.

I shoved down my briefs, exposing my hard shaft. She nibbled on the corner of her lips as she gazed at my erection.

I stroked my length, stopping at the head, squeezing.

"Tell me something, dirty girl. Have you ever sucked a cock before?" I knew the answer from her list, but I needed to hear it from her.

"No."

"How do you know you'll like it, then?"

She raised her chin. "Because I'm getting wetter just looking at yours."

I groaned to heaven and hell and back. How was I going to last with her? With this innocently filthy beauty.

My only chance was control. I had to wrest more of it from her, or I'd lose myself. I was already spiraling far too fast for my own good.

That was why I'd placed another toy order today. That was why I'd try to avoid her name too. If I used her name when we were intimate, we'd become Adam and Nina, when we were supposed to be the man who was number ten and the dirty girl. The virgin and her tutor —that was who we were when we worked through her list. Nothing more. I couldn't chance it.

"Open my gym bag," I said in my sternest voice. "Take out the paper bag on the side."

She let go of the grip on her wrists, reaching over and sliding open a side zipper on my bag. She murmured when she saw what was inside. "You bought this today?"

"It arrived at my office this afternoon. I washed it with soap and water. I wouldn't let anything touch your perfect body that wasn't pristine. Put it on while I watch you."

She rose, slid the pink straps over her luscious legs, then positioned the pink butterfly over her clit.

"Give me the remote, dirty girl."

She handed me the control.

"Now get on your knees, hands behind your back, and I'm going to feed you my cock."

"Oh God," she said, her shoulders trembling.

Yes, that was better.

The more I stayed firmly in control, the less likely was I'd lose myself to this gorgeous woman at my feet. I had to keep it together or those feelings would return, and there was no place for emotions.

She opened her mouth, gasping as I stepped closer, wrapped a hand around her head, and turned on the vibrator.

"Oh, Adam," she moaned, her face falling against my thigh, her hair touching my hard-as-stone length, my name sounding fantastic on her lips. *Too fantastic.* "That feels so good, but I want to taste you," she said, breathless.

This woman. She was going to ruin me.

"I know you do. And you're going to do both," I said, rough and smoky, like I had to be with her. "You're going to suck me off while I make you come with this toy. Consider this number eight on your list, with a little extra something just for you." I yanked her head back. "Open those lips and kiss the tip, like a good dirty girl."

She opened those shiny pink lips and darted out her tongue, shuddering as the butterfly buzzed against her clit. I upped the pressure one more level as she wrapped her lips around the head.

And I saw stars.

Bright, brilliant stars.

Already. From that first lick. "*Yesssss.* You know what to do," I rasped.

"Mmm. You taste so good," she whispered as she licked the head like I was an ice-cream cone.

My vision blurred as lust rippled through my every pore. So soon. Too soon. She was too good, and I was losing it.

"Tell me something," I said, fighting to keep the control in my voice.

"Yes?" she asked as she lavished flicks of her tongue down the underside of my shaft.

"How'd you learn to do that? Because you don't kiss a dick like that unless you've done it before or watched a lot of videos. And I want to hear it from you. I want the answer from your lips before I give you what you want," I said, hitting a button to level up the toy once again.

Her whole body shook. "Oh God. Adam. Oh God," she panted, barely able to control herself. Good. That was what I wanted. Nina, unable to keep it together. Nina, falling apart before me. "I watch videos. I learned online. I practiced."

"On what?" I asked, expecting her to say a lollipop or a banana.

"On my fingers," she answered, as she drew the head back in and I nearly exploded from the eroticism of that image.

"You practiced on your own fingers?"

She nodded as she opened farther, bringing me in another inch.

I wanted to thrust deep into her mouth and go crazy, but I needed to see this more. I pulled out. "Show me. Show me how you taught yourself to blow my ever-loving mind."

She raised her right hand to her mouth, inserted two fingers, and sucked them down to the first knuckle, then the next. My dick jumped, begging me to get back into the warm pleasure cave of her mouth. But Nina wasn't done. She added a third finger, showing me she could handle girth, then drew all three far and deep.

I burned everywhere. Flames licked my skin.

"That's enough," I bit out. "Now do that to me. Show your tutor what a perfect student you are."

Wrapping her hands behind her back once more, she opened her lips, and I gave her my length, easing in at first, watching her lips widen around my shaft. I stared at her gorgeous mouth on me all while she gazed up, looking for my approval.

Curling a hand around her head again, I gave her just that. "You're so deliciously good, my dirty girl. So damn sexy. And I love that you saved your mouth for me. And I'm going to reward you." I turned up the device another level, and her body trembled, her eyes hazy with desire as the butterfly hummed louder between her legs. But there were no more words from her. Because her mouth was full. "Now take it all. Take all of me like you know you want to."

She drew me in farther, stopping briefly to adjust. I

didn't let go of my grip on her hair. Didn't want to. And she didn't need it. She knew what she was doing, and I watched her as she willed her throat to take me down to the root.

When I felt her relax, I pushed in the rest of the way, sliding to the back of her throat. She gagged once, her eyes watering the slightest bit, which was insanely hot. But what was hotter was how she kept her lips tight around me.

I met her gaze, gentling my tone. "Can you take it, baby?"

I knew the answer before she gave it with a nod. She didn't want me to stop.

"Yes," I groaned, my eyes sliding shut. "Your mouth, baby. Your tongue. So perfect."

She was a sorceress, working her magic on me. Nothing had ever felt like this. Nothing had come close to Nina, my beautiful virgin, taking me so goddamn deep, I could feel electricity in my toes. Across my scalp. Everywhere. I was a power line, jolting from pleasure every damn second.

And as much as I wanted to let go and pump, I had to watch. I opened my eyes, savoring the slow, steady rhythm of her taking my length in and out, deep then shallow, my shaft sliding between her lips. It was the most erotic thing I'd ever seen. So was the expression on her face—like she was lost in the moment.

I could get lost too.

And I had to stay focused. Had to use words and control. I ran my fingers along her cheek. "Look at you. Look at you sucking me off just like you wanted."

I could feel her moan against me. She sucked harder, with vigor and lust in her brown eyes.

"I'm not going to look away, dirty girl. I'm not going to look anywhere but at your gorgeous face when you taste me coming down your throat for the first time. And I'm not going to pull out."

A tremble seemed to roll through her body, and she nodded.

"You're going to swallow, and I know you're going to love it," I said, picking up the pace as desire barreled through me, curling through my veins.

Her knees slid wider, and I glanced down. Holy hell. She was rocking her hips, thrusting against the butterfly as much as she could. My girl needed to get off.

"You must be aching. You want to come so badly, don't you?"

She nodded as she sucked.

"Are you close?"

Another nod. Another fantastically deep suck.

And I was done.

The pleasure in me snapped, breaking, as my climax started to rush through my body like a tornado. "Don't stop, baby. I'm coming."

My hand curled tight around her, and I fucked her sweet virginal mouth through my release. "Yes. That's it. Take it all," I urged her as I came, my whole body shuddering.

When I pulled out, she let go of her own hands, grabbed my hips, and cried out against me, "Oh God, I'm coming too. I'm coming so hard."

Like that, with her face against my thighs, her hands

clutching me, her body quaking, my sweet, dirty girl fell apart at my feet.

A few seconds later, I turned off the butterfly, tossing the remote on the couch. I kicked off my shoes; shed my jeans, briefs, and shirt; and scooped her up, carrying her to her bedroom. She moaned happily in my arms the whole time, enjoying the aftereffects of her own climax.

I laid her out on the bed, her silky hair spilling across the pillow, her body soft and pliant.

She was incredible, and my heart thumped harder as I drank her in. She was so fearless, so eager. And she gave herself so freely. I'd never experienced anyone like her before. And I wanted to experience all of her, again and again. That hammering in my heart grew louder, and I wanted to tell it to shut up, but I wanted to kiss her more.

So I did.

I dropped a kiss to her forehead, inhaling her scent.

She smiled.

Then I kissed her nose, and she murmured.

Then I placed one on her lips.

She sighed softly.

"You deserve another orgasm," I said, my head swirling with longing for her, for more of her. "You know that? That was so damn good. You deserve to come again."

I didn't give her a chance to resist. I moved down her body, slid off the vibrator, and kissed her delicious wetness.

"You are the sweetest thing I've ever tasted," I whispered as I wrapped my hands around her ass, cupping her cheeks, bringing her closer to my mouth.

"I am?" she asked, but there were no nerves in her voice. Only a lovely, warm sound, letting me know she liked the praise, wanted to hear more of it.

"You are perfection, and I need another taste of you. I need to have you all over my lips," I said, and for a second, it occurred to me that I was begging her. And it hit me too—I didn't care. She was worth pleading to. I'd get down on my knees for another taste of her.

Only I didn't have to. I didn't have to beg, because she gave. She gave all of herself. And that made me the luckiest man in the world.

"Have me, Adam. Please have me," she whispered.

And damn, that sent my heart into overdrive. That organ slammed against my rib cage, even as I caressed her slickness with my lips, devouring the evidence of her first climax.

I tried to ignore the beating inside my chest as she rocked against me, letting go, giving in once more.

No one could give in quite like this woman.

No one seemed to know her own desires like Nina.

No one had ever been this free in bed, and I loved every single second of being with her.

In and out of the sheets.

That thought kept appearing insistently, inconveniently. I tried to dismiss it again and again, losing myself in the paradise between her legs as I kissed her till she came again, wildly, loudly, bucking against my face.

Once she was done, I climbed over her, at full mast

again. I cupped her warm, flushed cheek, staring deep into her eyes, feeling myself fall once more.

Time to focus on the list. On the reason she created it in the first place.

I had to do what I'd planned to do.

But before I could speak, she asked a question I wasn't expecting.

18

ADAM

She propped herself on her elbow, her head in her hand. "Why do you call me different things? At different times?"

Her gaze locked with mine as she leveled me with a question I didn't want to answer.

I knew the answer. I was vaguely aware in the moment why I did it. But I also knew it wasn't purposeful. Sometimes the sweet names slipped out.

"What do you mean?" I asked, hoping to buy some time to figure out what the hell to say.

"Well, sometimes I'm 'dirty girl.' Every now and then, I'm 'sweet girl.' And then there are these times when you call me *'baby.'*"

It didn't take long for her to home in on me. The woman had laser vision. Except she didn't have to know what I meant by all of those terms of endearment.

"Is that so?" I asked, going for a flirty tone that didn't fit the moment. But I had to try.

She nodded and smiled, then she did something we

hadn't had much occasion to do. She touched me. She ran her fingers down my chest, playing with my chest hair. "When you're all dirty, dominant alpha, you call me 'dirty girl.' You say that most of the time," she said with a knowing grin as her fingers trailed farther south, feeling so damn good. "Twice you've called me 'sweet girl,' and it's when we're doing something really dirty. Like when you came on my face, and when you put your finger in my ass. And I think you do it to remind me that you like it really dirty too. That you don't see me any differently when we're doing that."

Damn. She was undressing me, and I was already naked.

I said nothing, just waited. I schooled my expression, even as her nails brushed across my abs, her touch electric.

"And then sometimes you call me '*baby*,'" she continued. "I haven't quite figured that out, but I think you say it in the heat of the moment."

There. She'd done it. She'd seen through me. All the way.

But she'd also given me an out, and I grabbed it, clutching on for dear life, flashing her an easy grin. "You figured me out, Nina. It's just the heat of the moment."

Her brow creased. "It is?"

I dipped my face to hers, pressed a kiss to her forehead. She closed her eyes as I whispered, "It's all so damn good with you that sometimes I'm not thinking. I'm just living in the moment of your list."

The list.

That was it. That was all this could be.

She nodded. "That makes sense. I'm living in the moment too. And every moment has been incredible." Her fingers roamed up my chest, then she looped her hands around my neck, playing with the ends of my hair. So simple, yet so intimate.

Hitting me once more in a way I hadn't expected.

My skin tingled. Just from her fingers along my neck.

"Adam," she said, and my name sounded like honey on her lips. Like all the sweetness in the world. Because that was who my friend was in bed. She was my sweet, dirty girl. My sexy virgin.

And she was *mine*.

"Yes?" I asked, fighting off the desire to use her name.

Her lips curved into a grin. "You know how you said you'd ask me again tonight? To give you my virginity?"

I swallowed roughly. Of course I remembered that. "I do." For a split second, the terrible thought flashed through my mind that she was backing out, that she no longer wanted this.

But then she threaded her fingers more tightly through my hair, brought me closer, and whispered, "You don't have to ask. I'm giving it to you. It's yours."

And that was when I knew how screwed I was going to be.

19

NINA

And so I was there. I'd reached number nine.

Goodbye, V card, hello other side.

I was walking down the Jetway to a plane that would whisk me to another hemisphere. One foot in front of the other.

I sat up in bed, lifted my arms over my head. "Will you take my shirt off?"

"Yes." He rose too, reaching for the thin fabric and whisking it off me in a flurry. He groaned when he stared at my breasts.

He brushed his fingers between them, running them along the curves. "I didn't spend nearly enough time worshipping these beauties last night," he said, shaking his head like that was a damn shame.

As he cupped them, it seemed like a shame to me too. My nipples hardened under his touch, and I arched into his palms. "Maybe my list needs addendums," I said softly, playing with that idea. I hated the thought of completing the to-do list.

"Maybe it does," he said, then he drew me in for another kiss.

His tongue skated inside my mouth, and his lips felt hot and desperate. Like he was taking this kiss for the road.

Like it would be our last kiss.

My shoulders sank at that prospect, and already my chest panged with missing *this*.

This connection.

This kind of touch.

Now that I'd had it, how was I to go without it?

I didn't want to return to the land of nothing. I wanted to stay here, tangled up in hot, sweaty, mind-altering bliss.

But the list wasn't about my future. It was about my present, and that was where I needed to live, and to live fully.

I shoved all thoughts of tomorrow out of my head and surrendered to the power of his kiss. To his passion. To his need. My back bowed as he kissed the breath out of me, just the way I wanted.

When he broke the kiss, his hazel eyes were rimmed with longing.

But it didn't feel sexual, strangely enough.

And he didn't gaze at me like the dirty after-dark man I'd discovered he was over these last two nights.

He looked at me as my friend, as the man I trusted, the man who cooked for me and needled me over fun facts. The man who had a key to my home.

But in a flash, the familiarity of the last few years vanished.

His irises shone darker now, with a look that was becoming familiar too, in its own way.

His bedroom eyes.

He shifted behind me, sliding a hand from the small of my back up my spine, sending shivers through me. When he reached my neck, he scooped my hair away, brushing kisses along my skin, then nipping. "As much as I want to spread you out on your back and have you wrap your legs around me, that's not what I'm going to do. Know why?"

"Why?" I asked, knowing the answer, but loving the game, savoring the questions.

"Because that's not what your list is about. You're not a missionary girl, and I am going to take you the way you want. *Fuck me hard, fuck me good, fuck me for the first time,*" he gritted out, reciting the words from my list.

"Oh God, yes," I said, sinking deeper into the moment.

"And you know how you want it. You scripted it. You wrote it down." His hand curled around my neck, gripping me tighter.

I gasped, knowing what was coming. "I want it that way. I want number nine."

His mouth found my ear, and his voice was rougher than I'd ever heard it before. More demanding. "Then say it. Say it out loud. Tell me how you want me to take you for the first time."

I shuddered, drawing a deep breath, needing fuel to say the words. But when you've spent all your sex life in your head, detailing your fantasies, building them, crafting them, and creating worlds around them, it turns out it's not that hard to give voice to them at last. "Push me down on the bed. Pin me in place so I can't move. Do it hard. And do it now. Please, Adam, do it now."

The sound that rumbled up his chest was animalistic. It was obscene, and it thrilled me. His desire rocketed mine to another level.

The pulse beating between my legs turned into a needy throb, an insistent ache to be filled.

"Say it again. Beg me," he ordered, pushing my face into the pillows.

My knees were tucked beneath me, my stomach arched, my breasts flat against the bed, my cheek against the pillow. I was under his control, and I was outrageously wet.

I wanted him to know how much. To see my desire. "Please, Adam. I'm begging you. I want you so much. I'm so turned on. I'm so wet I can't take it." I craned my neck to look at him, no easy feat since his hand was curled around me, pinning me in place. "*Please.*"

His eyes turned feral. "One more time, dirty girl. Give it to me one more time."

My body shook with desire. I ached everywhere, desperate for him to slide inside me.

"Please, Adam. Please!" I cried out.

And that was enough for him.

With his hand still wrapped around my neck, he moved between my legs, pushing my knees wider so they were tucked alongside my body. I was his. His to enter, his to have.

I was giving him myself, and he was going to take me to the other side of desire.

He rubbed the head against my wetness, and I ignited. A moan fell from my lips.

"You're so wet, dirty girl. So soft," he said, praising me.

I'd miss that too when it was gone—his praise. Because his bedroom compliments sent me to another world, and I was already living on an erotic cloud nine.

Maybe this was cloud nine thousand.

He pushed farther, breaching me, the head inside me. I tensed. This was it. My God, this was happening. I wasn't working a vibrator; I wasn't sliding the rabbit inside me. The real thing was different, so damn different.

And wonderful.

"You okay, baby?" he asked.

"I'm good," I said, then willed myself to relax again. I wanted this more than anything. "Don't stop, Adam. Please don't stop."

"*Never.*"

He pulled back, and I was empty for a second, but that second ended when he thrusted deeper, filling me a few more inches.

I felt my body stretching, adjusting.

Welcoming him.

Because that was what I wanted. To welcome him inside my body. All the way.

"More," I whispered, so eager, even if it hurt the slightest bit.

"You want it all, dirty girl? You ready for all of me now?"

"Yes," I said, breathless, trembling, my whole body brimming with need.

He lowered his body, covering me, then brought his lips to my cheek. "Then take it, baby. Take all of me."

And he thrust all the way in.

I cried out. From the momentary slice of pain. From the sensation of being stretched to the limit. But before he could even ask if I was okay, and I knew deep in my bones that he would, I cut in. "I'm good. So good."

And I could feel him smile against my skin, his voice soft as he whispered, "That's what I wanted to hear."

Then he moved in me, pulling back, pushing in, finding a pace, following my cues.

They weren't hard to read. I was an open book, moaning and groaning and panting out *yeses* and *just like thats* and *oh my Gods.*

At one point, he pulled out so far that only the tip was still in me, and I squirmed, begging for more of him. "*Please*," I cried.

And he delivered the most devastating thrust, filling me to the hilt, bottoming out inside me. He was so deep in me that it was as if we'd always been doing this, always been coming together. "Oh God, Nina," he groaned, sending a new wave of pleasure crashing over me.

It was the first time he'd said my name when we were naked. And I heard so much in it. Wishes and wants. Needs and desires. Or maybe I just wanted to hear that.

That had to be it.

I wanted to believe he felt the same things I did. That wild horses were running away with his heart too.

Maybe I needed to feel it in this moment.

And because I did, I needed something else entirely.

As my body sparked, I whispered his name against the pillow then asked a question. "Can you flip me over? I want to be on my back."

He stilled inside me.

He didn't answer at first. Only breathed hard, his cheek against mine.

He relinquished his hold on my neck, freeing me to move my face closer to his. I offered him my lips, believing in a new fantasy.

Believing in the possibility of us.

He drew a gasping breath, then he crushed my lips in a fierce, passionate kiss that felt so out of this world I wanted to cry. From the ecstasy of a kiss like that.

Seconds later, he broke the kiss, sliding out of me smoothly, then shifting me to my back.

In that position, I parted my legs for him. Wide, open, ready.

Yes, this was my new dream. To have him like this, where I could let myself fall deeper into the make-believe. Into the fantasy that we were coming together on another level.

I reached for him, lifting my arms to his shoulders, around his neck, bringing him closer.

I never thought I'd want sex like this.

This ordinary, normal, everyday position.

But it wasn't a want. It was an aching need.

And he filled it as he filled me, gliding back inside seamlessly, stretching my body to the limits.

He met my gaze, and the look in his eyes staggered me. The intensity, the passion written in them matched everything I felt inside.

Or maybe I was imagining it. Maybe I was writing that for him. Yes, that had to be it. I was creating a new fantasy and weaving it around us. I'd do well to remember it was only in my head.

I had to listen to my body, so I did.

As instinct took over, I wrapped my legs around him, and he swiveled his hips, rocking deeper. Our bodies melted together; our sounds mirrored each other. As we moved like this, in perfect harmony, I ran my fingers up the taut muscles of his back, over his toned biceps, and across his neck. I was committing the feel of him under my fingertips to memory.

I'd want to recall this moment forever, I was sure.

My hands became my camera, snapping shot after shot of him through the lens of touch.

And as pleasure radiated through my cells, sweeping across every molecule, the enormity of my choice flashed before me like a neon sign.

The sheer magnitude of the real choice I'd made echoed relentlessly inside me. Not the one to give up something I'd held on to dearly for twenty-four years.

But the choice to have sex with my friend.

Because it wasn't just sex anymore.

It wasn't a list now.

I was no longer ticking boxes, because as he lowered his body to me, his elbows at my sides, his chest slick and hot against my breasts, his lips inches from mine, I *knew.*

That to me—this was making love.

Awareness flipped a switch in me, and my body tightened as impending bliss coiled inside me.

"Adam, I'm . . ."

I couldn't finish.

There were no words.

I was there, flying over the cliff.

"Yes. Come for me, baby. Come for me now, Nina," he urged, and I fell apart beneath him, shattering into a million beautiful pieces as pleasure, radiant pleasure, flooded my veins.

And he chased me there, thrusting and pounding, losing himself too. Calling my name, endlessly over and over, until he was quiet and all I heard was the pounding of our hearts, beating together wildly.

Dangerously.

I had fallen in love with him. I'd broken the rules of engagement, and I'd have to fix that and fix it fast.

The list.

Focus on the list.

20

ADAM

I'd like to say that was unexpected.

The intensity. The passion. The soul-shattering intimacy.

But that'd be a lie.

I knew when I walked in here tonight that sex with Nina would be the most spectacular thing I'd ever experienced, and the hardest too.

Because how was I supposed to return to the way we were?

My chest ached for her. My mind wanted to engage with hers all the time. My arms longed to pull her into an embrace, and my mouth yearned to pepper sweet kisses over her cheeks, her eyelids, her hair.

That was the risk.

The risk we were supposed to avoid.

Hell, a mere twenty-four hours ago, we'd established the rules of engagement. They were crystal clear. The list. Os. Friendship.

Done.

That was it. That was all. We'd mutually agreed on the endpoint, and now we'd arrived at the moment when we were supposed to walk away.

In two nights, we'd worked through her whole list. My God, we were voracious, and the thought made me laugh unexpectedly.

"What's so funny?" she asked, and it occurred to me this was the first thing either one of us had said post-sex.

And I was still inside her.

Yeah. Time to deal with that issue.

"I'll tell you in a minute," I said, easing out of her, then heading to her bathroom for a washcloth. After warming it up under the water, I returned and cleaned her up, then myself. I set the cloth in the hamper and returned to my gorgeous beauty, who radiated bliss.

She glowed from head to toe, and I wanted to kiss her all over, from her toes with their emerald-green polish to her thighs, all smooth and lovely, to the hollow of her throat.

I ran my fingers over that spot, the divot in her neck. Such a vulnerable place on the body. Pressing a gentle kiss there, I answered her, "What made me laugh is how big our appetites are."

She chuckled beneath me. "Come to think of it, I haven't had dinner."

I raised my face, set a hand on her stomach. "My fault. I'll need to rectify that soon with paninis, melting cheese, and fresh mushrooms."

She let her tongue loll out like a dog.

"But what I meant was—we raced through your list, Nina."

"My God, we were ravenous creatures, weren't we?" she asked, and seemed to fix on a smile, her voice turning more chipper than I'd expected in this moment. "I was just thinking about the list too. How we plowed through it."

"We get gold stars for speed of execution," I said, wishing we weren't talking about the list but rather what comes after it. Or what *could* come after.

She tapped my nose. "No, Adam. I should give you gold stars all around. You made my dirty dreams come true."

The moment turned surreal.

Seconds ago, she'd been keening beneath me, breaking apart, calling my name.

And now that was all it had been.

A dirty dream.

A filthy fantasy.

Her list was a bucket list, a project to shed her virginity so she could focus again.

And here on the other side of her innocence, we'd resorted to what we'd always been.

Pals.

Joking.

Talking.

Having fun.

We weren't sharing sweet nothings or whispering confessions of unexpected emotions.

Get it together, man.

Besides, how the hell was I going to tell her what I

wanted? Did I even know? This Mack truck of feelings had slammed into me from out of nowhere, and I honestly wasn't sure how to sort them out.

Or, at this point, if I should.

Maybe we were well and truly done, with number nine under our belt.

Best to focus on that.

"You were a model student," I said with a grin, because now wasn't the time to let on that I wanted more than her list.

Or the moment to tell her that tonight never felt like a checklist item for me.

Yes, sure, technically we'd achieved her mission.

But, in doing so, something else had unfolded for me.

Something that wasn't on my list, or hers.

That was the trouble. Falling wasn't on the agenda.

And I didn't have a detailed plan for how to deal with it, how to broach it, or what the hell it would mean for us.

I focused on number nine instead, because it was easier. Running my fingers down her arm, I asked, "What did you think of number nine, sweet girl?"

Her lips curved up. "I'm 'sweet girl' now?"

I dotted a kiss on her nose. "You're always sweet to me." There, that was honest.

She ran her fingers through my hair, nibbled on her lip, then said, "Thank you."

"For what?"

"For doing that for me."

My brow creased. She was thanking me? I didn't

want thanks. I wanted her. Moreover, I wanted her to want me the same damn way.

Not in a *thank you for your service* kind of way.

I needed to devise a plan, to figure this out.

But how was I going to figure it out this close to her, when I was inhaling her sweet smell, drinking in her intoxicating scent?

"You don't have to thank me," I said, and I didn't know where I was going next, but I was going somewhere. "I wanted to do everything with you."

"You did?" Her tone pitched up, rising with hope like it had earlier when she'd asked if I'd liked going down on her.

Rap, rap, rap.

I blinked.

What was that?

The knocking sounded again.

She jolted out of bed, scrambling to her bureau, grabbing a T-shirt. "My door. Someone is here."

"Just ignore it." But as soon as I said that, the knocker called out.

"Mr. Larkin, it's David from City Painters. Just need a tiny minute of your time."

I groaned, my head falling back on the pillow for a long few seconds of frustration. I swung my feet over the bed, left the bedroom, and found my briefs, jeans, and T-shirt. In seconds, I was dressed, my phone in my pocket, and I answered the door.

David smiled proudly at me, his craggy face pleased. "We finished. Come see it. It looks fantastic."

"Thanks," I said. "Appreciate that. I can see it tomorrow."

"No. You have to see it tonight. My men can't clock out till the client gives approval."

I gritted my teeth, sighed heavily. "I've no doubt I'll approve it."

His grin widened. "We finished early. Bet you didn't think we'd finish it on Friday night."

"No. I sure didn't." And I wished he hadn't.

He tipped his forehead to my place. "Come. You'll want to see it before you sign off. You can pay tonight, yes?"

"Of course. Of course I can. Just give me a second," I said, and returned to the bedroom to find Nina in yoga pants. She'd brushed her hair and knotted it into a bun. Her laptop lay on the bed.

It was as if we were erasing the evidence, rewinding to casual buddies who helped each other out with guest rooms for crashing in and food for noshing. "I need to go see what's going on next door."

"Yes, go. I hope it looks fabulous. I need to"—she paused, like she was thinking—"I need to prep for tomorrow. I had a last-minute booking with a client who's in town with her lover this weekend. She's doing some casino-themed shots, so I need to go over my plans to shoot her in a bed of coins."

I ached a brow, laughing. "That's interesting."

She shrugged with a smile. "What happens in Vegas stays in Vegas. You know how it goes."

Then she winked at me, as if the city's slogan was ours. As if it was a reminder that we were a secret.

Was that all we could be? Nighttime rendezvous and dirty deeds, midnight trysts and secret fantasies?

I wanted to know what number eleven was. Wanted to ask if we could write in numbers twelve, thirteen, fourteen, and more.

It had felt like she'd wanted that too.

But hell, maybe I was wrong. Maybe she responded the way she did because it felt good. Because she had a little kinky sub in her, and I gave her my kinky dom.

Maybe that was it.

My mind raced, hunting for answers in her eyes. I didn't find any, so I crossed the distance, curled a hand around her head, and kissed her lips.

When I broke the kiss, I told her I'd be back later. Because that was how it worked. I should return.

I *would* return.

"See you then."

But David wouldn't shut up. "Let me show you the finish close up," he said, guiding me from room to room. "We are masters at detail. Take a look at this." He pointed to the doorway of the guest room, where my parents would stay next week.

"Terrific."

"You won't get that from anyone else. You chose well. That is why we had to spend the extra time. You won't regret it."

But I was already regretting having answered the door.

"No regrets for the paint," I said, flashing a *thanks and we're done* grin.

He chuckled and clapped me on the back. "That should be my new corporate mantra." He sighed deeply, pleased, then snapped his fingers. "Let me just have you sign off on the invoice."

"Great." That was what I wanted, so I could return to Nina.

He reached into his bag for a clipboard then flipped through some pages, whistling under his breath. He found mine and took his time tugging it gently from the holder.

Kill me now.

I snagged a pen from the counter, and the second the paper was free, I scrawled my name.

"Now, just a little green and we'll be good."

I located my platinum card, and he slid it through a card reader. But the credit card company decided to be a douchebag and spent its sweet time verifying that this wasn't fraud.

I mean, that was all well and good, but was tonight the time for Chase to call and verify I was me?

Evidently.

Thirty minutes later, David left, my condo still smelling of fresh paint.

Nina would be hungry, and I needed to feed her, not to mention find a way to figure out what the hell to say.

But when I returned to her apartment, the place was quiet. A stillness floated through the air. An empty protein bar wrapper was on the kitchen counter.

I padded to her bedroom.

My heart raced to my throat. There she was. My sweet Nina, curled up on top of the bed, her laptop open, her yoga pants and T-shirt on, sound asleep.

Good sex had a way of doing that to you. It was the best medicine for an excellent night of rest.

I lifted the corner of her covers, tucked them diagonally over her, and dusted a kiss to her forehead.

Her breath came steadily. *In, out, whoosh.*

I tried on her name in the faintest of whispers, too soft to wake her, but needing to test it.

"Nina, I fell in love with you."

Her breath stayed at the same pace, and I turned out the lights, left the room, and shut the door.

Tomorrow I'd have to find a way to say it for real.

I did not want to be startled awake by the Rolling Stones. Not now. Not at this godforsaken hour. Because it could only be a disgustingly early time of day.

I squinted, reaching for my phone next to me on the guest bed.

Morning light shone through the blinds, the sun blaring its arrival. Grabbing the phone, I silenced Brandon's ringtone then answered.

"Hello," I grumbled.

"*Bonjour!* Also, where is my parade? My motorcade? My marching band?"

I groaned. "My bad. Forgot to order one."

"I forgive you, I suppose. Well, as long as you pick me up at the airport."

I scoffed. "There is this thing called Uber. You download it, use it, and it takes you everywhere."

"I know. Just messing with you. I'm in my Uber now,

on my way to your place. The only room I found was a master suite at the Bellagio for two grand a night, so I'm all yours today. See you in ten."

I sat bolt upright. "See you."

Scrubbing a hand across my jaw, I tried to make sense of my day, and how my plans had been upended. Well, technically I didn't have any plans till tonight when the crew would hit our favorite spot at The Luxe, but I needed to work, go to the gym, see my sister, and, oh yeah, one more thing. Find a way to tell Nina I had fallen for her without, y'know, screwing our friendship.

That was all.

I dragged myself out of bed, peered down the hall, and saw her door was still closed. I wandered over and pressed an ear to it. I didn't hear any stirring. My sexy angel was still asleep.

And that sucked.

In the guest bathroom, I took a piss, brushed my teeth, washed my face, and then pulled on my clothes from last night.

Her home was still painfully silent as I padded to the living room, images of what we'd done there last night flickering before me.

My friend on her knees, waiting for me.

Nina taking me in her mouth.

My sweet, dirty girl losing control on the butterfly.

My shaft twitched, like a dog longing to be let out.

But it would have to get in line.

I headed to her kitchen counter, spotted the owl notebook, and grabbed a sheet of paper, scribbling out a quick note.

. . .

Brandon is here, and I need to go. And you said you have a client. But I want to see you later. I need to see you later. And don't forget—we're all going out tonight.

I don't know how I'm going to look at you without thinking of how absolutely beautiful you are on your knees, on your stomach, on your back.

In every way.

You're beautiful—my sweet, dirty girl.

P.S. Did you know Antarctica is the only continent where pumpkins don't grow? Lucky Antarctica.

There. That wasn't too much. It was just enough for where we were, but it hinted at more. More something. More us.

I left the note by the coffee pot, a surefire guarantee she'd see it.

Then I set the pen by the notebook.

This notebook.

And to think this was where it had all started. I ran my finger down the cover, as if it had magical powers and would tell me how to win Nina's heart, along with her body.

I flipped it open to her list, smiling as I reread every item.

And then I saw a new one.

My skin turned electric.

She'd filled in number eleven.

21

NINA

I was alone, and it was fitting.

I'd always done well with my own company, processing my day, sorting my thoughts. After last night and all that had happened and *hadn't* happened, I needed time to figure out what to do next.

I padded out of the bedroom, but the open guest room door and the lack of Adam's phone and gym bag told me he was gone. I knew he was busy today, so I wasn't worried. I'd shower, have some coffee, and prep for my shoot.

I headed for the bathroom and cranked up the heat. I lifted my face to the water, letting it beat down on me. A mere twenty-four hours ago, I'd luxuriated in the water then too, the newness of my sexual explorations a palpable thing.

I supposed they were this morning too.

After all, last night I'd crossed the bridge.

But as I ran my hands down my body, I still felt like me.

I felt the same.

I was the same woman I'd always been.

Because the woman I was had always wanted sex, wanted kink, wanted submission in its own way.

Now, I was simply the woman who'd had those things.

Was I different?

I turned around under the water, shampooing my hair.

The difference, I supposed, wasn't in my body and whether someone had or hadn't entered it.

The difference lay in *who* I'd let in.

Adam was inside me in a deeper way. When he'd touched me for the first time, it was like he was breaking down a wall. One I hadn't known I'd erected. One that had prevented me from seeing him in certain ways. Before he found my list, I'd assumed he was the sweet guy next door, a fantastic friend. Charming, confident, and 100 percent a good guy.

He was still all of those things. But he was more. So much more. He was my filthy match. And if I hadn't taken the chance on working through my list with him, I'd never have known that we'd set each other on fire in the bedroom.

I trembled as memories raced past me.

We were an inferno in bed. We were wild together. We melted into each other. And that told me more than an awkward post-sex conversation about lists and gold stars did.

I had no prior evidence. No point of comparison.

But in the bright light of morning, I knew I didn't need one.

Because I was certain in my body and in my heart that we'd shared something deeper than a laundry list. The connection was real, visceral, and powerful.

Yes, the moments after sex had been weird, with me trying to keep it light.

But I didn't linger on those images.

I scrolled through the viewfinder on my mind's camera to *before*.

When we were naked, looking into each other's eyes, falling apart. He'd said my name, something he hadn't done before. He'd said it over and over, and he'd sounded like a man who'd lost himself too. Lost himself to emotions, to possibilities, to a future like this.

Was it too much to hope for? Too much to ask?

I didn't know, but I burned with longing. A new kind of longing—I craved a deep intimacy, and I craved it with my best friend.

After I rinsed the soap from my body, I turned off the water and stepped out of the shower.

Brushing my teeth, I reached for my phone on the vanity and scrolled through the recent episodes of *Ask Aphrodite*, finding one that fit my state of mind.

The title was *True Intimacy—How to Ask for It.*

I hit play, and that smooth, sensual voice filled the room.

Hello there, gorgeous lovelies. Today we're going to tackle a different side of sensuality. But it goes hand in hand with sexual exploration. After all, doesn't true intimacy in the bedroom come from intimacy outside of it? Rare is the couple who can set fire to the sheets without the foundation of love, respect, and adoration. In fact, I will die on this hill: great sex is only possible with great love.

And as you've been learning how to ask for what you want inside the bedroom, I urge you to ask for what you want outside of it too.

It's far too easy to stay where we are, in our comfortable places, and never take a chance.

But a chance at true intimacy is a chance worth taking.

I know. I've been there, and I want you all to have what I've had.

So, if you're on the cliff, jump off. It's worth it.

I won't give you a step-by-step instructional. All I will say is, you won't get what you want unless you ask for it.

I hit end, stared at myself in the mirror, and vowed to find a way to ask. After I dressed for my shoot, my stomach rumbled and my brain demanded coffee.

I answered the call of the belly and the brain and headed for the kitchen, where I stopped short. There was a note left by the coffee maker.

My heart stuttered. Nerves slammed into me.

But then I talked back to them. After all, I'd been learning how to ask for what I wanted.

"Please let this be my chance."

I opened it.

22

BRANDON

For the record, I was not a cheap bastard. I'd looked far and wide for hotel rooms.

I'd happily pay a couple hundred a night for one on the Strip. No. Make it an even five.

But I couldn't find one for less than two grand.

When certain conventions sent more than one hundred thousand people at any given time to Sin City, one did not simply find a hotel room that didn't cost a kidney the night before he flew to town.

Still, that was what friends were for, and I was damn glad I had Adam and his offer to turn to when I got off this plane.

But first, champagne.

The blonde flight attendant handed me a glass. "It's calling your name, Mr. Winters."

"But it's so early," I said playfully, shaking my head as if truly debating the consumption of this beverage. "How can I live with myself for drinking so early?"

"It's not early in France," she said with a wink in a

faint French accent. "Pretend you are at your favorite brasserie, having a glass, watching the men and women walk by on cobblestoned streets."

Ah, sounded exactly like my life for the last few years.

I raised the glass, grateful the airline had upgraded me, thanks to my frequent flyer miles. "When you put it like that, how can I live with myself for *not* drinking this champagne at three in the afternoon in Paris?"

She patted my shoulder, smiling softly. "Exactly."

It was a passing touch. It ended a second later as she moved to the row behind me, treating another first-class passenger to a breakfast drink.

But it was enough to remind me of how long it had been.

Three years of only passing touches.

Three years of missing.

Three years of watching the world go by.

I lifted the glass and downed half the drink, letting the bubbles tickle my nose and go to my head.

I wasn't going to get drunk on half a glass of champagne. *Please.* But as the plane zoomed closer to Vegas, the city where I'd met, romanced, and fallen madly in love with Jenna, I'd need a drink or two to get off this plane.

Hell, I'd required shots, lots of shots, last time I came here.

I downed the rest of the glass for good measure.

When the attendant turned around, passing me again, she didn't ask if I wanted another. Instead, she stopped, giving me a soft grin. "What brings you to Vegas?"

"Friends. Work. The usual."

She arched a curious brow. "And is that good?"

"Good enough," I said, my standard reply.

"Sometimes 'good enough' is all we can hope for, isn't it?" Her brown eyes were rimmed with sadness. She didn't even try to hide it. It was there to see so easily, to read so completely.

But then, that was what I did. I read people. "Yes. Sometimes it is all there is."

She sighed, a little melancholy sound, but then she smiled, and just as quickly, her sadness disappeared. It was gone in the snap of the finger. "But we go on, and we find the joy in other things, don't we? That's what I've done."

I was too startled by the slice of honesty she'd served up to say anything at first. It was rare to connect with a stranger so easily, one I knew I'd never see again.

But maybe that was what strangers were for sometimes. For those unexpected encounters that cut you right to the heart.

"Yes, I think that's true," I said. "At least, I hope it's true."

"It is," she said reassuringly. "I'm finding mine again. I'm trying again. You'll get there. I can see in your eyes that you're thinking about it. I know you'll get there, and you'll be glad when you tried."

She set her hand on my shoulder once more, took my empty glass, and walked to the galley.

It wasn't romantic, her touch. I didn't follow her to

the galley and beg for her number. That wasn't what that moment was about.

It was about something more.

About letting go.

This stranger, who could read loss in my eyes just as easily as I'd seen it in hers, was an unexpected comrade in arms, giving me permission to let go.

And as the plane began its descent, diving toward the city that once belonged to my heart, maybe that was exactly what I needed.

It was only a weekend.

But maybe it was time to let go.

When I reached Adam's condo, he yanked open the door and clapped me on the back in a quick hug.

"Good to see you," I said, filling with a new sort of happiness—the kind that came from seeing old friends. It was a centered, balanced kind of joy.

His brow creased. "You look different."

"It's Botox. Shh. Don't tell anyone," I said as I moved past the doorway.

"Ah, that's it. Did you have those collagen injections too?"

I set down my bag and laughed from deep within.

Adam tilted his head to the side. "Yeah, you don't usually laugh like that. What's up? Because it isn't Botox."

I took a beat, my laughter fading. "I didn't expect

this to happen. I wasn't looking for it. But I had this strange sort of moment."

"What happened?" he asked, leaning against the kitchen counter, curiosity in his eyes.

I told him about the flight attendant and he nodded, listening thoughtfully. "And that's what you needed, that sort of permission almost? To move on? Like a final step?"

"Yeah, I think so," I said, wrapping my head around this morning, understanding it fully now. I tapped my sternum. "I mean, who knows what tomorrow will bring, but I feel this lightness in my chest I haven't felt in ages."

"Maybe sometimes all we need are those chance encounters that help us see what we've been missing," he mused.

"Maybe so," I said, and this was why Adam and I had stayed friends over the years. We could shoot the breeze, talk about business, and dive deep when we needed to. "But enough about me. How can I thank you for letting me crash here?"

A slow grin took over his face, and he ran a hand over his jaw. "Well, there is this one thing."

23

NINA

The shoot lasted all day, thanks to Vegas traffic.

There were no two ways about it. On convention days, you needed to charter a hot-air balloon to make it anywhere on the Strip in under an hour.

Unfortunately, I didn't have those kinds of funds.

But I did have fabulous clients, and Chantal—for all her idiosyncrasies and her bed of coins—was one of them.

Because she knew what she wanted. A true lady boss, the olive-skinned beauty laid down the law.

"First, I want a shot of me in the elevator, lost in thought, wearing my little red dress."

Done.

"Then, I want you to capture me walking down the hallway to the hotel room."

Check.

"And then, you go into the room and take pictures of me entering the suite, like I'm getting ready for him."

Finished.

"And finally, I want all the seductive shots of me on the bed."

And that was where I was now, taking her picture as she posed in a sea of coins, like she owned this moment.

"I'd love it if you could run a hand through your hair with your head falling back," I told her from behind the lens.

"Like this?"

"Nailed it," I said, then took those shots.

When I showed her the preview on the back of my camera, she hummed over each and every image. "These are divine. My husband will love them."

"No doubt he'll be enthralled."

"I hope he gets the meaning too," she said, a little quirk in her lips. "But I know he will."

"I would love to know the story behind these photos. Will you tell me?"

"We met in Vegas years ago. Here in this hotel. A one-night stand that turned into forever. I want him to see these and know I still want him as much as I did that night when he won one thousand dollars at the slots and took me back to his suite."

"You're the true riches," I said, understanding fully. I learned so much from my clients. Every one, it seemed, had something to impart about femininity, sexuality, or confidence. I had the best job in the world. "And I love that you're showing him through photos. That you're communicating your passion through images."

And she gave me an idea.

* * *

At Lily's home, I pawed through her closet, hunting for a simple dress. She lived closer to the Strip than I did, and I didn't want to rush back home to change and shower before we met the guys at The Luxe.

"Ooh! Go for the purple one. You always look good in purple," Kate said from her spot on the bed, nursing a glass of red wine.

"I do love purple, though this one looks a bit skintight," I said with a wink. "Do you only own dresses that require shoehorns to fit into?"

"Hey! I have some that aren't."

Kate snorted. "Maybe one."

Lily simply shrugged and raised her wine glass to her lips, taking a sip. "I enjoy those dresses."

"And Finn does too," Kate chimed in as I sorted through more clothes, stopping at a fuchsia dress with a neckline that dipped to the belly button, leaving little to the imagination.

I held it up. "Trivia question. This little number was on Lily for how much time before Finn ripped it off?"

Kate thrust her hand in the air. "Five minutes!"

Lily mimed hitting a buzzer. "Oh, so sorry. We're going to need you to phrase that in the form of a question."

"What is five minutes, Alex?" she asked, as if Lily were the *Jeopardy!* host.

In a pitch-perfect imitation of the man, Lily replied, "No. The correct answer is *What is five seconds?*"

I bowed before her. "Impressive. But it does raise the question—why do you ever wear clothes with him?"

"Yes. I'd like to know that too," Kate put in, kicking her leg back and forth.

"I often ask myself that as well," Lily said, then her eyes snapped to her closet. "How about the green one? All the way in the back. I actually haven't worn it yet."

I raised a brow. "A virgin dress."

Kate cleared her throat. "And I believe that raises another question . . ."

"Is the virgin dress for a virgin?" Lily asked.

I reached for the emerald number, slid it off the hanger, then turned around. "No, it's not for a virgin. It's for me."

The squeals could split eardrums.

"You've been holding that in for the entire time you've been here," Lily said, then smacked my shoulder. "Shame on you."

"Tell us everything," Kate said, patting the bed and taking another drink.

I sat, but I didn't tell them everything. I told them hardly anything. I was still a private woman with private fantasies. I would keep most of them to myself, and my partner.

And I hoped that partner would always be Adam.

"And it was incredible," I said, finishing the Spark-Notes version. "So incredible that you were right, Lily. When you told me to be careful."

"Oh, sweetheart. Are you okay?" she asked, placing a hand on my arm.

"I'm fine. I'm great actually. But I wasn't careful with my heart, though I think that might be for the best. I have a plan. I was listening to another episode of the podcast this morning—"

Kate sat up straighter, her eyes gleaming. "I started listening to that too. Serena is great. That's her real name. She has a fascinating background and personal story. She brings so much of herself to the show," she said, enthused as she shared more details on the hostess who'd been my guide through intimacy. "But enough about her. What has she inspired you to do tonight in that emerald dress?"

Something even more daring than the other items on my list.

Something that would require both my body and my heart.

And a whole dose of crazy confidence.

24

ADAM

The music pulsed low at Edge, our crew's favorite club in the heart of The Luxe Hotel.

Brandon and I were the first to arrive, and we snagged a spot on a velvet couch that the ladies loved. With scotches in hand, we talked about his favorite neighborhoods in Paris, then the best new restaurants in Vegas, before we segued to interesting stories in the news and the world. Books, politics, work, life—we touched on all of it, and more when Jake and Finn joined us.

Jake covered drinks as he'd promised to do, and we toasted when the waiter brought a fresh round.

"To new business," Jake said, then tipped his forehead to me. "And to doing business with friends. May it always go so well."

I clinked my glass to his. "And even though you always give me shit, there's no one I'd rather have inking my deals."

Finn cleared his throat, chiming in, "So proud of my protégé. I taught Jake well."

Jake laughed, shooting Finn a look. "Yeah, I'm your business partner, asshole. Not your protégé."

"Details. Details," Finn joked, then dropped the teasing. "Best damn business partner ever. And friend."

Brandon raised his glass. "And let's drink to old friends."

"Hear, hear," I said.

We all toasted to that once more. Finn and Jake had been good friends for years, like Brandon and me. And good friends were the guys you could ask to do anything, as I'd done with Brandon earlier.

A few minutes later, the ladies arrived. Lily strode in first, and Finn stared hungrily at his wife.

Kate followed Lily, and Jake gazed at the tall, willowy brunette like he wanted to tear off her clothes. Nina appeared next, and when my eyes landed on her, my heart hammered against my chest.

This woman had turned my mind upside down in forty-eight hours. The night I'd found her list, I'd still been stalled in my Rose-induced time-out. I was Mr. Thanks But No Thanks when it came to trust. I didn't want to take a chance with anyone who could stab me in the back.

But then Nina showed me what trust truly was. By opening her innermost thoughts and deepest fantasies to me, and only me. By letting me be her guide through her wild, dirty dreams.

I'd thought I was the teacher, showing her how to have all her filthy fantasies.

Turned out, she'd been teaching me all along.

How to trust again.

How to fall again.

How to open my heart to the woman who was meant to be mine.

Vulnerability.

Intimacy.

Love.

I'd never seen that trio coming, but as Nina walked toward me, exquisitely sensual in an emerald dress that hugged her curves, I saw all that and more.

I saw everything in her.

Before she could reach us, I rose, walking past the other patrons, my eyes only on her. When she was inches from me, I held her face. "You," I whispered, then I kissed her lips, tasting forever on them.

I'd intended to ask her for number eleven.

I had it all mapped out. How I'd tell her, how I'd let her know she'd stolen my heart.

But when you're kissing the woman you've fallen madly in love with, you don't always want to wait for the perfect time to tell her.

Not when she'd roped her arms around my neck as she gave her mouth to me, asking with her body to be kissed fiercely, passionately.

And with ownership.

That was what my Nina had wanted from a man.

That was what she wanted from *this* man.

To be taken.

And hell, was I ever taken with her. So damn taken that when I broke the kiss, I couldn't wait. "I'd like to think that kiss made it clear, but I've learned from you that words matter. That spelling out wishes and wants is so damn important." I took a beat and gazed into her deep brown eyes as I clasped my gorgeous woman's face. "So let me say this—I broke the rules of engagement."

A grin played across her pink lips, and she whispered, "Me too."

That emboldened me, but then, I was already feeling bold tonight. "I broke the most important one of all."

"You did?" Her voice was a little flirty, but full of so much hope—a hope I felt deep in my soul.

"I broke it, and I don't want to fix it because I don't want to go back to friendship with you."

"I don't either."

"I want to have everything with you. I want to be your man, your lover, your person, and your friend at the end of the day."

She trembled, her voice hitching. "I want all of that too."

I ran my thumb across her cheek. "And in case it wasn't clear, I am wildly, madly, deeply in love with you."

"Oh, Adam, I'm so in love with you." One lone tear slid down her face, but before I could kiss it away, she brushed her lips with mine in a soft, tender kiss.

A kiss only she could give me.

And in it, I felt *her* ownership.

Of my heart and my soul and my whole damn mind.

It was everything I couldn't live without.

When she broke the kiss, my head was hazy, and my

mind was racing to where I wanted to go, to what I wanted to say.

But she beat me to it, surprising the hell out of me when she said, "But there's one more thing on my list. I want number eleven."

I'd never left a place so fast in my life.

25

NINA

This wasn't how I'd planned it.

My goal was to show him how I felt.

But he'd beat me to it.

And I was good with that, so good. I didn't know how long I'd be able to keep the words inside me anyway. They'd been bubbling up in me all day long, then tangoing on my tongue the second I'd walked into the club.

Saying them at last was both relief and freedom.

And I hoped the rest of the night would be too.

When we reached my place, I told him I needed a few minutes to get ready.

"Take your time," he said.

"You probably want a glass of champagne though," Brandon added, since we weren't alone. He was with us, and he waved in the direction of Adam's condo. "I picked up a bottle for you two lovebirds earlier today. I'll go get it."

When he left, Adam followed me into the bedroom,

moving behind me when I reached the bureau, kissing the back of my neck. "You good with this? With him being here?"

I turned around so he could see the truth in my eyes. "Yes. I've wanted this so badly. I started to write it on my first list, but wasn't sure if I could go through with it."

"What changed your mind? I have to confess, I saw it there this morning, but I love that you asked for it this time."

And this time, I wasn't bothered that he'd looked at my list again. He *was* the list, and the list was *us*. It was ours. "What changed is when I started to fall for you. That's when I wanted it even more."

He banded his arm around my waist, pulling me closer. "You know I never want another man to touch you."

"I know that," I said with a naughty smile. "And I don't want anyone's hands on me but yours. That's why I want the camera to capture us. I want to see how we look together. I want to be on the other side of the lens," I said, my breath catching in my throat as I gave voice once more to my newest, most erotic wish. "I want to be seen as a woman in love and in lust. I need to know what that looks like when we're in bed. And I want it with you and only you."

He groaned, his eyes sliding shut as he yanked me close and kissed me.

Then he left the room, letting me undress and dress again alone.

I could have asked one of my boudoir photographer colleagues. But I hadn't realized till this morning that I was ready to show Adam through photos how I felt for him. And I didn't know how Adam would react.

But Adam was ready too.

He'd already asked Brandon to be behind the camera.

He trusted Brandon, and therefore I did too. Besides, we'd be using all my equipment. Brandon would have nothing to take away from the session but memories. I'd keep the photos.

I didn't want to shoot them myself, because I didn't want to break the mood to set up the pictures. I wanted to be captured in the act, to see how I looked in the throes of passion, to see in myself what I'd been imagining in my clients for so long.

I touched up my hair and makeup, dressed in white panties and a matching bra, and grabbed a glass of champagne from the kitchen counter. I took a drink and headed to my studio to make sure my camera was ready.

I set down the glass on a table in the corner.

Then I posed.

On the edge of the bed in my studio, my body sliding off the mattress, my back and shoulders on the covers, my head to the side, away from the door.

One arm slid down my body, settling on top of my panties. The other was in my hair.

I could hear my heartbeat in the quiet. It pounded in my ears, a drumbeat of desire and want.

A few seconds later, the door opened.

"Hi there." It was Brandon, his boots clicking across the hardwood floors.

"Hi," I said, but I didn't break the pose.

"He's not going to know what hit him, Nina. With you like that."

I smiled at the compliment. It wasn't sexual. It was professional, from one person who worked behind a camera to another.

And it came, too, from someone who knew Adam well.

"Thank you. And I want to see how that looks."

"He's so crazy for you," Brandon added, and from the sounds, I could tell he was behind the camera, probably peering through the lens. "I hope this gives you everything you want."

I was sure it would, especially once Adam entered the room. He drew a sharp intake of breath. He came to me, kneeled on the soft white rug at the foot of the bed, and brushed my hair from my cheek.

Click.

"Hey, sweet girl," he said, a tender whisper.

"Hi, Adam."

Then the scene began.

I moved up on the bed, sliding seductively along the covers. Wearing only black boxer briefs, Adam followed, stalking me on his hands and knees, like an animal hunting for his meal.

I was easy prey, and we liked it that way.

We didn't pose like my clients did. I didn't want staged photos. And I didn't want only the *before*.

I wanted it all, and I wanted it real.

That was how Adam gave it to me. He was completely raw and real as he covered me with his body, raising my arms above my head. "Hold onto the headboard, dirty girl."

Click.

I did as he asked, my body burning hotter as he used that name for me.

That was who I wanted to be for him right now—his, and only his, dirty girl.

Then he shifted to my side, the camera seeing my whole body as he moved down me, kissing the hollow of my throat, my shoulders, the tops of my breasts. I moaned, arching against him, as he unsnapped my bra.

Click.

I didn't feel an ounce of shame or embarrassment over the camera capturing our intimacy. I felt only pleasure, only trust.

With my breasts bared, Adam nuzzled his face between them, kissing at first, then nibbling. Next came a nip on the sensitive flesh.

I yelped, but it was chased by an *oh* as he soothed the bite with a lick.

Then he raised his face, met my gaze, and stared hotly at my lips. "Bet you'd like me to come on these beauties, dirty girl."

"Oh God, yes."

He rose, kneeling, cupping both my breasts, squeezing them together. "Bet you'd love it if I fucked these perfect tits and came all over your throat."

I moaned my *yes,* at his words and at his rough touch that I loved.

"Put that on your list. Number twelve. You're making a new list, dirty girl, and we're going to work our way through all of it, over and over."

Tingles spread down my body, settling between my legs, where I ached for him. "I want that with you. I want to do it all with you. I want you to have me in every way, Adam."

Click.

Brandon was only taking pictures. There would be no video with this. No words to return to and play again and again. No soundtrack to listen to. But when I looked at this image later, I was sure I'd remember the words perfectly. *Have me in every way.*

I wanted that with this man, my after-dark Adam.

His hands traveled along my sides, down to the waistband of my panties. "I'll give you everything, my sweet, dirty girl."

"Yes. God, yes. Have me." I arched my hips, asking.

"That's it. Beg me with your body," he said roughly, moving his thumbs under the band.

I rocked my hips higher, harder, thrusting at him. "Please give me your mouth. I love your tongue, love your lips."

His groan echoed across the room as he pulled down my panties, exposing me.

There was no click.

Not until Adam moved between my legs, burying his face in my wetness. Then I heard it. Another click, mingled with the sound of my first feral moan.

It wouldn't be my last.

As I moved against his mouth.

As I arched against his lips.

As I parted my legs wider.

He wrapped his hands around my ass, scooping me up, lifting me impossibly closer to his wicked, wonderful tongue.

Pleasure charged through me, surging across my body, taking me in a storm of bliss.

Yes, *bliss.*

I was in it. I was having it. And later, I'd see it.

But right now, I was living all my fantasies, and reality was so much better as I lost control with the man I loved.

I let go of the headboard, writhing, my hands in my hair, on my breasts, on my face.

I was caught in the throes of the most intense climax of my life, as Adam devoured me till the waves subsided.

But then, the moment grew more intense. Adam rose, shed his briefs, and kneeled next to me, stroking himself near my face, before he let go to bend close and whisper in my ear, "I love you so much, Nina."

A second wave of pleasure crashed over me at those words. "I love you too," I whispered.

"Now let's show the camera how much." He adjusted me, pulling me up and shifting me so I faced the camera on all fours. He moved behind me, spread my cheeks, angling me higher, then he pushed inside my wetness.

I cried out, my neck stretching, my hair spilling down my back.

Click.

Yes, this was what I wanted. Everything exposed.

Everything seen, as the man I'd fallen in love with me took me in a whole new way.

Without reservation.

He'd never held back with the physical. But now he was fully free too—to speak uninhibitedly as he fucked me rough and with passion. Whispering filthy things to me. "Grind against my shaft, my dirty girl. Show me how much you love it when your man fucks you hard."

My body pulsed for him. I ached for another climax.

"I love it when you fuck me," I cried out, rocking with him as he thrust harder, deeper. "Because I love you."

He grabbed my hair, yanked hard, and covered my back with his chest as we moved together, him now doing most of the work. He brought his lips to my ear, his words low and just for me. "I know you do, baby. I feel it all with you. I have every single time."

And I lost it again.

I lost myself in him, peaking and soaring into another climax, one that stole through my body at record speed.

But as he followed me there, groaning, cursing, and chanting my name, I knew neither one of us were lost.

We were both found.

And we'd been seen.

26

BRANDON

I'd be lying if I said I wasn't aroused.

I'm only human.

And I'm a red-blooded man who likes sex.

No, who loves it.

Plus, there was that nagging issue of my dry spell.

Three years long.

So yeah, I was turned on AF behind the camera.

Which was admittedly a little weird.

My best friend was starring in a homemade porn.

But I knew better. This wasn't porn. It wasn't for someone else's titillation. And it wasn't staged.

Nina didn't moan like an actress begging to be banged by the biggest dick in the room.

She clearly only wanted Adam. She never cheated to the camera, never tried to show a better side, or a dirtier side.

He was the same, his focus only ever on her.

And I'd seen my fair share of porn. Online videos had nothing on these two. The camera revealed the depth of their feelings for each other as I caught shot after shot of their passion. The look on her face, the intensity in his.

That said everything. And it said all the things porn never did.

It was the truth.

They came together like it was their only truth—the way they felt for each other.

And when they finished, and they curled up, softer, gentler, tangled in each other, I snapped that too. They'd want that—the before, the during, and the after.

Because it was the *after* that spoke the loudest. That said who they were to each other.

They were so madly in love that something else in me cracked.

Maybe it was the last layer of pain. The last layer of self-protection.

I hadn't come to Vegas looking for absolution from grief.

But somehow, absolutely unexpectedly, I'd found it on a plane, and it had been finished in a bedroom as I witnessed someone else's love. As I saw everything I'd denied myself since Jenna died.

And as I learned something new about myself.

I didn't want to be lost after her.

I wanted to move on. I wanted to live again. Someday soon.

27

ADAM

A week later

That was a helluva day.

One of my new shows had started production, and I'd had a fantastic meeting with a pair of business partners.

I was giving today an A-plus already. I didn't even need to wait for the night to update my grade book. Nights with Nina were always an A-plus.

Even though I wouldn't be able to get my woman alone till much later.

My parents were arriving at the airport any minute, flying in from North Carolina where they'd been enjoying their retirement.

I met them at baggage claim, smiling broadly when I spotted the two of them on the escalator, hand in hand.

My mom laughed at something my dad said, then he tucked a strand of hair behind her ear and kissed her forehead. Seeing them like that, more than thirty years after they'd said *I do,* warmed my heart.

I was a lucky guy. I loved my family, enjoyed the company of my parents, and had great friends.

And I wanted *that* too—right in front of me.

Someday soon, I wanted *that* with Nina.

For now, I walked over to the escalator and brought them both in for hugs once they stepped off.

"Good to see you, Mom, Dad."

"Good to see you too, son," my dad said.

"And you look quite happy," my mother added, scanning my face. The woman missed nothing. "Any particular reason for that?"

"There's a very particular reason for that," I said as I walked to the carousel. "And you're going to meet that reason tonight."

My parents loved Nina. No surprise there. She was engaging, smart, and loved to ask questions.

So did my mother, and the two of them gabbed all night long over our sushi dinner, talking about modern art, new shows to see in Vegas, and quirky scientific discoveries. That was my Nina.

As the brunette beauty reached for a piece of rainbow roll, she said to my mom, "You should definitely check out this new podcast I've been listening to."

I froze.

She wasn't going to mention *Ask Aphrodite* to my mom, was she? Nina had told me about it, but even though Mom was cool, she didn't need to tune into something that had helped my girlfriend ask me to push her face into the pillows and screw her hard.

Something I did nightly, *thank you very much*.

"It's all about modern art, and the hostess dives into whether any of it has meaning at all," Nina said.

I relaxed, laughing quietly to myself.

Of course she wasn't going to say anything.

Some things were private.

What we did after dark and why would always be one of them.

Later that night, with my parents sleeping soundly in my newly painted condo, I joined Nina in her bed.

That was where I'd spent every night for the last week.

And tonight we had a new item to tackle on our list.

Number twelve.

Seemed fitting to add it officially, since we'd talked about it in the heat of the moment.

Tonight I gave her that, something she wanted, and something I wanted too.

After, when we cuddled, I found myself counting the days till I could ask this wonderful woman to be my wife.

Was tomorrow too soon?

The answer was yes. It was definitely too soon.

But a month later, I'd arrived at a different answer.

Nina had asked me to join her on a passion project, as she called it. When she wasn't shooting empowering images of women feeling beautiful, she was drawn to the natural world. To landscapes, deserts, and forests. We didn't have forests in Vegas, but outside the city, we had a beautiful desertscape in Red Rock, with its canyons and rock formations.

Today, we hiked through it as Nina took photos. "Some new ones for our wall," she said, because I'd moved in with her and put my newly painted place up for sale.

"You don't want to hang those photos of you in your white panties on the wall?" I teased as I followed behind her on the path.

She lowered her camera and swiveled around. "Those are only for us."

"I know, baby. And I love looking at them with you."

That was an item on our list we checked off over and over, because we both loved those pictures. They were so goddamn arousing, the visual record of our love, our intimacy.

They were decadent, dirty, and endlessly erotic.

And I was so damn glad she'd asked for number eleven, because her boldness in asking for what she wanted bolstered me today.

I planned to ask for what I wanted most.

After we hiked to a picnic spot, she set down her camera and I spread out a blanket. "Sandwiches for my sandwich monster," I said, and her eyes lit up. Nina loved to be fed.

"Are they going to make me sing a rock anthem?"

"I do believe they will make you croon. But first I need to ask you something."

"Ask me anything, Adam," she said, so open, so trusting.

God, I loved this woman.

She made it so easy to get down on one knee, meet her gaze, and give her all my truth. "Nina Bellamy, you are the most wonderful, giving person I've ever met. You've been my friend and my lover, and you've shown me so much about trust and faith and love," I said, my heart expanding to fill my whole damn chest.

Her eyes shone, tears glimmering in them.

"And the only other thing I want is for you to be mine always. Will you be my wife?"

She nodded as tears streamed down her cheeks. "Yes, Adam. Yes, I'll be your wife. I've only ever been yours, and I'll only ever be yours."

And that was the most wonderful gift.

I slid a gorgeous solitaire on her ring finger, then kissed my bride-to-be as passionately and fiercely as I ever had.

There were no engagement photographers. No photos captured by someone else for social media.

But I had the record of this moment etched into my mind, and it was perfect.

It was real, and it was ours.

And it always would be.

BRANDON

A few weeks later

My second shoot for the watchmaker in Los Angeles had been another success.

So good in fact that the client upgraded me to first class for my return flight home to Paris.

I wasn't going to complain.

Not when I settled into the plush leather seat in the second row. Not when I checked the menu for the flight, my mouth watering over the offerings. And not when I saw the wine list.

A glass of pinot, a good meal, and a long nap as I crossed the country and then an ocean. Sounded like a perfect plan for the flight. I'd been enjoying the little things in life more, and this sure as hell counted.

I closed my eyes, settling into my seat, savoring a little moment.

Then I heard a voice.

One I'd been hearing since a certain flight a couple of months ago.

I'd thought she was just a stranger. That was the role I'd assigned to her.

But I couldn't get the flight attendant out of my head. Her advice had touched down deep inside me. I wanted to remember her words, to hold on to them, so I'd memorized her voice.

You'll get there. I can see in your eyes that you're thinking about it. I know you'll get there, and you'll be glad when you tried.

And there was that voice again.

"Can I get you a drink before we take off, Mr. Abernathy?"

My eyes snapped open as she asked the man in front of me for his beverage order.

As if on cue, her gaze traveled to mine. She blinked, then a sliver of a smile tugged at her lips. She returned her focus to her customer, who asked for a bourbon.

A minute later, she brought it to him, then she moved to stand by my seat, a knowing grin on her pretty face. "And what brings you to Paris this time, Mr. Winters?"

My smile spread of its own accord. She remembered my name. "Just heading home."

"What a coincidence. I live there too. Another American in Paris."

I sat up straighter, feeling buzzed with possibilities for the first time in ages. "You never told me your name."

"You never asked."

I smiled at the beauty in front of me and let her own words be my guide. *You'll be glad when you tried.*

"I'm Mr. Winters, as you know. But my friends call me Brandon. And I'd love to know your name."

Her smile was radiant. "I'm Miss Parker. But my friends call me Serena."

A few months later, I opened the mailbox at my flat, fishing around for bills or letters. I found an invitation. One I'd known was coming.

I turned and showed it to the woman by my side.

The woman who'd become my lover, my partner, and my friend.

Serena Parker moonlighted as a flight attendant, but her passion was helping others find deep love and intimacy through her podcast.

She was like me. She'd loved and lost, but she was on the other side now.

So was I, and I was loving life with this woman. We spent our free nights together, dining at off-the-beaten-path restaurants, wandering along curving roads lit by streetlamps, and imagining the places we'd travel together. We'd go to faraway islands, eat pineapples, and watch the sunset. Or we'd travel to remote lands, embarking on long hikes that led us to beautiful vistas.

And this time, we'd return to a place I knew well. A place I wanted to go with Serena.

"Would you like to go to a wedding in Vegas with the best man?"

She arched a sexy brow. "I very much would."

EPILOGUE

Ask Aphrodite

Hello, my gorgeous lovelies! I've been reading your comments and enjoying your questions.

I love that you have so many, and they remind me of how many paths there are to love and intimacy.

I've noticed, too, quite a plethora of questions about me.

Who is the woman behind Ask Aphrodite? Who is the woman who guides you through the wilds of desire and sensuality, wherever you are in your journey?

I'm like all of you. And I'm like myself again.

We all have our own stories to tell.

Mine is that I've found a second chance.

And I'm here to say that great love is possible more than once.

I've found it with a new man, and he's found it with me too. Do we have it all? I'd like to think so. Because I practice what I preach. I practice openness and honesty and communication.

That, my lovelies, is the heart of what this show is all about.

Learning how to ask for what you want.

If you ask for it, you just might get it.

As for me, I'll be signing off for a few weeks, since we're heading to a certain city to attend the wedding of a good friend. And while I'm there, we'll be eloping, and then flying someplace warm and tropical, where we'll make love all day and night.

And we'll eat pineapples too.

ANOTHER EPILOGUE

NINA

"You look beautiful."

The words came from my sister, Ella, as she raked her eyes over me in my wedding gown.

"So do you," I said, giving her the same treatment in her black maid-of-honor dress. "Also, I think you might be next."

"Shh," she said, bringing her finger to her lips. "Don't jinx me."

Ella had met a fantastic man, a single parent like herself, and they'd been going strong for some time now.

"There is no jinxing when it comes to love," I said as she handed me my bouquet.

"Enough about me," she said, dismissing the conversation, her expression turning serious. "I have to tell you something important. Something I've hoped to be able to say for a long time. I want you to know I'm so glad you waited. And I don't say that because of me. I say that because of you. You're so happy with Adam, and all I've ever wanted is to see my little sister this incandescent."

That's how I felt today, and every day with him.

"Thank you," I said, emotion clogging my throat.

She shot me a stern stare. "No crying. Not till you're Mrs. Adam Larkin."

I couldn't wait to be his officially.

But truth be told, I'd been his since that first night when he found the list.

As I walked down the aisle, Miss Sheridan beamed, whispering, *"I knew it,"* when I passed her. I smiled back, and then my eyes were only on the beautiful man waiting for me, as he watched me walk to him. I felt radiant, knowing we had a lifetime of lists and love ahead of us.

When the justice of the peace pronounced us man and wife, Adam drew me in for a deep, possessive kiss.

Yes, this was the man I'd fallen for.

And now he was my husband.

My always.

Later that night at the reception, it was time to toss the bouquet.

I faced the other way as the single women gathered behind me. On the count of three, I sent my bouquet of daisies flying. I expected to see Ella clutching it, but I was shocked to turn around and find the flowers in the hands of a very surprised Kate.

While Jake stared at her knowingly.

That was interesting.

I'd have to find out what that was all about.

But tonight was mine and Adam's, so I pulled my husband in for a dance, thrilled to be in his arms where I belonged.

THE END

Did you enjoy Nina and Adam's sexy love story? There's more in this world! Jake and Kate have a story to tell and it's coming soon in THE DECADENT GIFT. Don't miss the release! **Be sure to sign up for my mailing list for the After Dark line to be the first to receive this sale alert!** Sign up for my VIP After Dark mailing list here!

Did you enjoy **THE VIRGIN GIFT**? Please leave a review on Amazon! Also, if you're looking for more high-heat titles, check out NIGHT AFTER NIGHT and NIGHTS WITH HIM! If you're looking for a sexy romantic comedy, grab ASKING FOR A FRIEND!

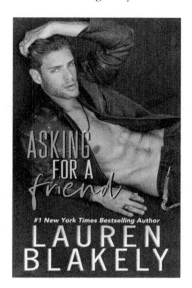

ACKNOWLEDGMENTS

Big thanks to Lauren Clarke, Jen McCoy, Helen Williams, Kim Bias, Virginia, Lynn, Karen, Tiffany, Janice, Stephanie and more for their eyes. Goddess love to Helen for the beautiful cover. Thank you to Kelley and Candi and KP. Massive smooches to Laurelin Paige for access to her brain and heart. As always, my readers make everything possible.

ALSO BY LAUREN BLAKELY

FULL PACKAGE, the #1 New York Times Bestselling romantic comedy!

BIG ROCK, the hit New York Times Bestselling standalone romantic comedy!

MISTER O, also a New York Times Bestselling standalone romantic comedy!

WELL HUNG, a New York Times Bestselling standalone romantic comedy!

JOY RIDE, a USA Today Bestselling standalone romantic comedy!

HARD WOOD, a USA Today Bestselling standalone romantic comedy!

THE SEXY ONE, a New York Times Bestselling standalone romance!

THE HOT ONE, a USA Today Bestselling bestselling standalone romance!

THE KNOCKED UP PLAN, a multi-week USA Today and Amazon Charts Bestselling standalone romance!

MOST VALUABLE PLAYBOY, a sexy multi-week USA Today

Bestselling sports romance! And its companion sports romance, MOST LIKELY TO SCORE!

THE V CARD, a USA Today Bestselling sinfully sexy romantic comedy!

WANDERLUST, a USA Today Bestselling contemporary romance!

COME AS YOU ARE, a Wall Street Journal and multi-week USA Today Bestselling contemporary romance!

PART-TIME LOVER, a multi-week USA Today Bestselling contemporary romance!

UNBREAK MY HEART, an emotional second chance USA Today Bestselling contemporary romance!

BEST LAID PLANS, a sexy friends-to-lovers USA Today Bestselling romance!

The Heartbreakers! The USA Today and WSJ Bestselling rock star series of standalone!

The New York Times and USA Today
Bestselling Seductive Nights series including
Night After Night, After This Night,
and *One More Night*

And the two standalone

romance novels in the Joy Delivered Duet, *Nights With Him* and Forbidden Nights, both New York Times and USA Today Bestsellers!

Sweet Sinful Nights, Sinful Desire, Sinful Longing and Sinful Love, the complete New York Times Bestselling high-heat romantic suspense series that spins off from Seductive Nights!

Playing With Her Heart, a

USA Today bestseller, and a sexy Seductive Nights spin-off standalone! (Davis and Jill's romance)

21 Stolen Kisses, the USA Today Bestselling forbidden new adult romance!

Caught Up In Us, a New York Times and

USA Today Bestseller! (Kat and Bryan's romance!)

Pretending He's Mine, a Barnes & Noble and

iBooks Bestseller! (Reeve & Sutton's romance)

My USA Today bestselling

No Regrets series that includes

The Thrill of It

(Meet Harley and Trey)

and its sequel

Every Second With You

My New York Times and USA Today

Bestselling Fighting Fire series that includes

Burn For Me

(Smith and Jamie's romance!)

Melt for Him

(Megan and Becker's romance!)

and *Consumed by You*

(Travis and Cara's romance!)

The Sapphire Affair series...

The Sapphire Affair

The Sapphire Heist

Out of Bounds

A New York Times Bestselling sexy sports romance

The Only One

A second chance love story!

Stud Finder

A sexy, flirty romance!

CONTACT

I love hearing from readers! You can find me on Twitter at LaurenBlakely3, Instagram at LaurenBlakelyBooks, Facebook at LaurenBlakelyBooks, or online at LaurenBlakely.com. You can also email me at laurenblakelybooks@gmail.com

Printed in Great Britain
by Amazon

33425695R00129